"Go away, Leah."

John's voice lashed like a whip across the room, halting her in midstep. He was ready for a fight. More than that, he wanted one. But why?

"John, please, I've come here to help—"

"I don't *want* or *need* your charity," he muttered. "So why don't you grab your suitcase and just get the hell out of here," he said with a quiet emphasis that almost had her scurrying to obey.

"I'll get out of your study...for now. You're obviously in the midst of a self-indulgent wallow of some sort, and I might as well leave you to it. But I'm not getting out of your house, not tonight or tomorrow or the day after that. I never knew you could be such a jerk, John Bennett," she finished, unable to keep the hurt from her voice.

"There's a lot you don't know about me, Leah," he warned softly, turning to face her. "A lot you don't want to know. Believe me."

Dear Reader,

Make way for spring—as well as some room on your reading table for six new Special Edition novels! Our selection for this month's READERS' RING—Special Edition's very own book club—is *Playing by the Rules* by Beverly Bird. In this innovative, edgy romance, a single mom who is sick and tired of the singles scene makes a deal with a handsome divorced hero—that their relationship will not lead to commitment. But both hero and heroine soon find themselves breaking all those pesky rules and falling head over heels for each other!

Gina Wilkins delights her readers with *The Family Plan*, in which two ambitious lawyers find unexpected love—and a newfound family—with the help of a young orphaned girl. Reader favorite Nikki Benjamin delivers a poignant reunion romance, *Loving Leah*, about a compassionate nanny who restores hope to an embittered single dad and his fragile young daughter.

In *Call of the West*, the last in Myrna Temte's HEARTS OF WYOMING miniseries, a celebrity writer goes to Wyoming and finds the ranch—and the man—with whom she'd like to spend her life. Now she has to convince the cowboy to give up his ranch—and his heart! In her new cross-line miniseries, THE MOM SQUAD, Marie Ferrarella debuts with *A Billionaire and a Baby*. Here, a scoop-hungry—and pregnant—reporter goes after a reclusive corporate raider, only to go into labor just as she's about to get the dirt! Ann Roth tickles our fancy with *Reforming Cole*, a sexy and emotional tale about a willful heroine who starts a "men's etiquette" school so that the macho opposite sex can learn how best to treat a lady. Against her better judgment, the teacher falls for the gorgeous bad boy of the class!

I hope you enjoy this month's lineup and come back for another month of moving stories about life, love and family!

Best,

Karen Taylor Richman
Senior Editor

Please address questions and book requests to:
Silhouette Reader Service
U.S.: 3010 Walden Ave., P.O. Box 1325, Buffalo, NY 14269
Canadian: P.O. Box 609, Fort Erie, Ont. L2A 5X3

Loving Leah

NIKKI BENJAMIN

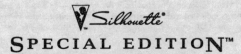

SPECIAL EDITION™

Published by Silhouette Books

America's Publisher of Contemporary Romance

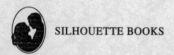 SILHOUETTE BOOKS

ISBN 0-373-24526-2

LOVING LEAH

Copyright © 2003 by Barbara Wolff

This edition published by arrangement with Harlequin Books S.A.

Visit Silhouette at www.eHarlequin.com

Printed in U.S.A.

Books by Nikki Benjamin

NIKKI BENJAMIN

was born and raised in the Midwest, but after years in the Houston area, she considers herself a true Texan. Nikki says she's always been an avid reader. (Her earliest literary heroines were Nancy Drew, Trixie Belden and Beany Malone.) Her writing experience was limited, however, until a friend started penning a novel and encouraged Nikki to do the same. One scene led to another, and soon she was hooked.

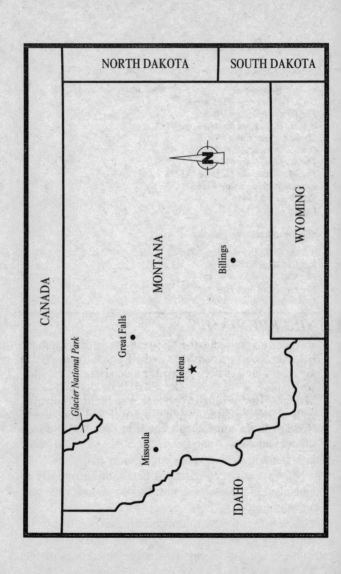

Chapter One

In her modest sedan, Leah Hayes could have covered the distance from her father's spacious home to John Bennett's house in a matter of minutes. And on almost any other occasion, she would have done so without a second thought. Despite the eight years she had been away, the tree-lined streets of the neighborhood, within easy walking distance of the University of Montana campus in Missoula, were still familiar to her. But with her reception so uncertain, Leah chose to take her time.

"Are you lost, Aunt Leah?" her six-year-old niece asked, her soft, sweet voice edged with anxiety.

"No, Gracie," Leah assured her, smiling ruefully as she glanced in the rearview mirror. "I remember the way to your house."

Gracie's frown eased, though only just a bit.

The little girl looked like both her mother—Leah's stepsister, Caro—and her father, her features a perfect blend of the two. From Caro, Gracie had gotten her heart-shaped face and silky blond curls, and from her father, John, she had inherited the grave, pale gray eyes and determined tilt of chin that Leah had tried so hard, and so unsuccessfully, to forget in the years she'd been away.

"But you're driving really slow," the child pointed out.

"I'm admiring all the pretty flowers." True, but not the whole truth behind her dawdling. "Everyone seems to have worked really hard on their gardens this year."

"Not us." Gracie's disappointment sounded in her voice. "All we have in our flower beds are scraggly old weeds."

"Well, that's something we can fix while I'm here. Pulling weeds and planting flowers won't take us any time at all if we work together."

"Maybe my dad could help us, too," Gracie murmured wistfully. "Before my mom died he always used to make sure we had pretty flowers."

"Maybe so," Leah agreed, though she had no idea at all what John would or wouldn't be willing to do in the weeks ahead.

"He'll probably be too busy," the child said with an audible sigh of resignation. "He's always too busy to do things with me, or he's too sad. He really misses my mom, you know. But you're here now, Aunt Leah, and you'll do lots of things with me, won't you?"

"Oh, yes, Gracie. I'm here now, and we'll do lots and lots of things together this summer. I promise," Leah said, making yet another vow to someone she loved before she'd had a chance to consider what it might cost her.

"See all the weeds in our flower beds?" her niece said as they turned onto Cedar Street.

"Yes, I do," Leah replied, trying to hide her dismay at how run-down and abandoned the lovely, two-story house appeared compared to the photographs Caro had so proudly sent her a couple of years ago.

With the streetlights illuminating the house, she gave it a closer look. Though not totally weed-infested, the gardens were overgrown, the lawn could have used a good mowing, and the front windows were all dark despite the onset of evening.

She had hoped her father and stepmother had been exaggerating about John's mood and behavior. Surely he had begun to get over the worst of his grief and was now ready to move on with his life again. He had responsibilities that couldn't be ignored, Gracie being the most important among them. And he *had* agreed to let her help him take care of his daughter for the summer, hadn't he?

"Do you think my dad's home?" Gracie asked as Leah turned into the driveway, the uncertainty in her voice adding to Leah's own.

"That's his SUV, isn't it?"

"Yes," the little girl replied, then added by way of explanation, "but that doesn't mean he's home. He goes for long walks at night. Really, really long walks, and it's nighttime now."

Leah could understand John's avoidance if she'd been the only one showing up on his doorstep. But would he go for one of his long walks on an evening when he was supposedly expecting his daughter to come home, as well? The man she had known eight years ago wouldn't have, but John had changed after Caro's death in ways that Leah wouldn't have believed possible had anyone except her father told her.

"If your father isn't home, we can always go back to Grandpa's house and wait there until he returns," Leah said, hoping she sounded more decisive than she felt.

"Okay," Gracie readily agreed, her fears obviously eased by Leah's simple solution.

Deciding to leave her suitcase in the trunk of the car, Leah helped Gracie out of the back seat. The little girl had only a slight bit of trouble maneuvering her injured leg, encased in a metal brace, so that she could stand up, but she accepted Leah's assistance graciously. And though she was more than capable of walking up the brick path that led from the driveway to the front door of the house on her own, she also tucked her hand into Leah's. Leah held on gratefully, receiving her own measure of reassurance from the physical contact.

Pausing on the small covered porch, she took a deep breath, gave Gracie's hand an encouraging squeeze and rang the doorbell. A cool breeze stirred the tree branches and lifted her straight, shoulder-length brown hair as she listened to the faint echo of the chimes. Shivering slightly, she wished she had put on her sweater before leaving the car. It might be June, but in Montana the night air still held a definite chill that her jeans and denim shirt couldn't ward off.

"Oh, no…" Gracie murmured as seconds ticked into a minute, then two, without the door opening.

Reaching out, Leah pressed her finger against the doorbell a second time, holding it there several seconds longer than she had the first time. Another minute or two passed and then, to her relief, she heard the sound of the bolt lock being drawn.

"He's here!" Gracie's voice was filled with an odd

mix of excitement and uncertainty that Leah determined to be a consequence of her father's erratic behavior.

Choosing to ignore as best she could the quiver that stole along her own spine, Leah forced herself to smile. The simple words "Hi, stranger" formed in her mind, a perfectly acceptable greeting after eight years, especially if spoken in a cheerfully teasing tone.

The front door finally swung open, not smoothly but with a jerk that signaled impatience, even irritation, and in the semidarkness, the man looming on the threshold presented a frightening visage, at least to Leah's eyes. Had she not expected him to be John, she would have never recognized the person now standing before her.

With his dark, shaggy hair unkempt, his face unshaven, his eyes bleary, his navy T-shirt and faded jeans hanging much too loosely on his tall, lanky frame, John Bennett looked no more familiar to her than a total stranger would have. And a hostile stranger at that, she thought, her smile fading and her jaunty greeting left unspoken.

"Hi, Daddy," Gracie said.

The child's high, sweet, hopeful voice filled the gaping silence as she let go of Leah's hand and took a tentative step forward.

Immediately John's expression changed, softening perceptibly as his gaze shifted to his daughter. His love for the little girl was so obvious and unencumbered that it seemed almost palpable to Leah. Here was the man she remembered, she thought, the good, kind man who would never intentionally hurt anyone, especially her. He wasn't hostile at all, only ravaged by a grief so profound and desperately unrelenting that nothing, save the sight of his beloved daughter, could ease it.

"Hi, Gracie." John bent down and scooped his

daughter into his arms, gently cradling her injured leg in one large, competent hand. As he straightened up, he shared a warm and heartfelt hug with her. "Did you have a good time at Grandma and Grandpa's house?"

"Oh, yes. They had a big surprise for me, too." With a satisfied smile the little girl turned and waved a hand at Leah. "Look, Daddy, it's Aunt Leah. You remember her, don't you? I went to visit her in Chicago with Mommy a whole bunch of times. Now she's finally come to visit us here in Missoula, and guess what? She's going to stay right here with us all summer, and I'm so glad, Daddy. Aren't you?"

"Of course I remember your aunt. In fact, I remember her quite well," John replied in a noncommittal tone, his gaze settling on Leah. "Welcome back to Missoula, Leah."

She started to smile again, started to greet him as she'd planned, but the expression on his face belied his softly spoken words. Though not openly hostile, the glance he cast her was, at the very least, unfriendly. So unfriendly, in fact, that it caught her completely by surprise. And his failure to agree with Gracie that he was glad she would be staying with them spoke volumes about his feelings in that regard, as well.

She had thought that John was not only aware of the arrangements her father and stepmother had made on Gracie's behalf, but that he also approved of them. He had to have known that she was the one Cameron and Georgette had chosen to serve as the little girl's nanny for the summer. Surely they'd discussed their plan with him and gotten his approval before approaching her, hadn't they?

But if John *had* given his approval, why was he treating her with such hostility?

Leah realized that she'd never asked either Cameron or Georgette how John felt about the matter, and apparently, in their wisdom, they had chosen not to mention it themselves. They had told her only that John had changed quite a bit since Caro's death, and to Leah that had been understandable, considering the extent of his loss. Had she known he would be irritated by her arrival and dislike the idea of her living in his house, she would never have agreed to return to Missoula.

What had possessed her to assume so much, so mistakenly?

Her love for Gracie, Leah realized. Cameron had insisted that John was still too preoccupied with his own loss to give the little girl the attention she needed, and Gracie's comments in the car had verified that. And then, of course, there had been that unavoidable flare of hope, coupled with the sudden reawakening of long-dormant dreams, that had stirred deep in her soul at the thought of seeing her dearest friend again after eight long, very lonely years.

She hadn't expected John to share her feelings. Barely a year had passed since Caro's death, and he would never love anyone as much as he'd loved her. But neither had Leah anticipated such a total lack of warmth, not to mention welcome.

"The nanny's room is on the far side of the den past the kitchen," he directed, interrupting her reverie in a no-nonsense, matter-of-fact tone of voice. As if she was a lowly stranger hired for the summer against his better judgment, instead of someone with whom he'd once shared his hopes and dreams, Leah thought, staring at him in undisguised bewilderment.

"Make yourself at home," he added, his cool, distant expression devoid of any hint of invitation. Then to Gracie in a much softer, gentler tone he said as he turned away, "I bet you had dinner at Grandma's house, didn't you?"

"Oh, yes, my favorite—hamburgers and French fries."

"Well, then, let's get you upstairs and into your pajamas. It's almost past your bedtime, young lady."

Putting her arms around her father's neck, Gracie giggled with uninhibited delight.

Standing alone on the porch, watching John walk slowly up the staircase just inside the entryway of the house with Gracie held close in his arms, Leah's first impulse was to yell, "Hey, wait a minute. Where do you think you're going?" She couldn't do it, though. Not with Gracie looking on. The little girl deserved a peaceful night's sleep, and she definitely wouldn't have one if she first had to witness an angry scene between her father and her aunt.

But Leah had a right to know what *was* going on with John. She'd had what now seemed to be the glossy version from her father and stepmother. Apparently they had given her just enough information—distinctly shaded to the positive—to lure her back to Missoula. And with her guard down, she had been totally unprepared for the problems they must have known she would surely encounter.

Of course, she couldn't claim to be totally innocent. She had gone along with the plan easily enough, she acknowledged, fumbling along the wall inside the doorway for the switches that turned on the porch and entryway lights. She'd believed what they'd wanted her to believe because she'd wanted to believe it, too.

Her father and stepmother had needed her help—help she'd been easily able to afford to give during her summer vacation. They'd been sure that if anyone could deal with John's moodiness while also providing a stable home for Gracie, it was she. And with her experience working as a teacher at a private girls' school in Chicago, Leah had known she could also help Gracie catch up on the schoolwork she'd missed due to her injuries.

Ruefully, she now considered all the questions she hadn't asked Cameron and Georgette, and remembered, much too late, all the words they had used to describe John Bennett—bitter, angry, not himself—which she had originally chosen to ignore. There had even been a comment about John running off two nannies in the past nine months—a comment she should have questioned more closely, but of course hadn't.

Obviously they hadn't left because he'd been nice to them, Leah acknowledged as she walked back to the car to retrieve her suitcase. And he certainly hadn't been nice to her, either. But she wasn't just any young woman hired through a professional agency to look after his daughter. She was Leah—his once and always friend. Or so she'd believed until he'd dismissed her without so much as a backward glance.

She could leave of course. She could just get into her car and drive back to Chicago. No one would blame her, not even her father and stepmother. But who would look after Gracie then? Who would care for the little girl as willingly and lovingly as she would? Not Cameron and Georgette—they were leaving for her father's summer lecture series in Europe early tomorrow morning. There wasn't anyone else Leah could think of.

So she would have to stay—or live with more guilt than her conscience could bear. But she wasn't going to tolerate open animosity from John Bennett, she vowed as she opened the trunk of her car. She shouldn't have to. He had been her friend once—her very best friend—and she was there for a very good reason.

As she had every intention of reminding him once she'd had a chance to gather her courage and stand up to him.

Chapter Two

"Are you angry with Aunt Leah, Daddy?" Gracie asked, her concern evident in the hush of her voice and the frown furrowing her brow.

Mentally cursing himself for upsetting his daughter on her first night back at home, John tightened his hold on her and gave her a quick kiss on the cheek.

"No, Gracie, I'm not angry with your aunt Leah," he said as they made their way up the staircase to the second floor.

Well, not any angrier than he'd been with anyone else intent on interfering with his life lately, he admitted to himself, not counting Gracie of course. But then, his daughter wasn't any interference at all, never had been, and to his way of thinking, never would be. From the moment of her birth, she had been the light of his life.

"But you sounded kind of growly when you talked to her, Daddy," Gracie insisted.

"Growly, huh?" he replied with a wry smile.

What a way she had of describing how he'd sounded! He smiled slightly, musing that his verbal release had resulted from the unfortunate mix of emotions he'd been experiencing all afternoon. Since Leah's father had first advised him earlier that day that Leah was the so-called nanny they had found to help him look after Gracie for the summer, John had been angry and resentful and, to his consternation, oddly unsettled, as well.

He was used to the anger. It had gone hand in hand with the pain of losing Caro in such a tragic, senseless, unexpected way. Resentment, too, had been a good friend in the months since his wife's untimely death. He didn't want sympathy, because to his way of thinking he didn't deserve it. He, and he alone, had been responsible for Caro's death. He had earned every agonizing moment he'd lived since that fateful night, and then some.

The restiveness he had been battling the past few hours was something else altogether, though—a feeling he most definitely didn't want to indulge in, especially in regard to Leah Hayes.

A heart thrum of tension had lanced through him at just the thought of having her in his life again on a daily basis—close enough to see, to touch. He'd wanted to roar like the caged and wounded beast he'd felt himself to be for far too long. When he'd actually had to open his door to her and meet her clear, level gaze face-to-face for the first time in eight years, he'd been stirred by a nearly uncontrollable urge to pull her into his arms, hold her close and confess, without any constraint, the many sins he'd committed.

It was lucky for all concerned that he had only come across as "growly." And he would have to put a lid on even that particular tone of voice, at least whenever Gracie was around, he thought as he set her down just inside the bathroom doorway and switched on the overhead light.

"Yes, Daddy, *very* growly," she assured him. Then, tugging at his hand, she added gravely, "We can go back to Grandpa and Grandma's house if you need some more private time. Only, we'll have to come back here again tomorrow 'cause somebody else is going to be staying there while they're gone on their big trip."

Squatting on his heels in front of his daughter, his heart twisting at the painfully tentative look in her eyes, John smoothed a hand over his daughter's tumble of blond, silky curls.

"I'm so glad you're home again, Gracie, even if I didn't exactly sound like it when I came to the door. And you're staying right here with me from now on," he vowed. "I've had enough private time the past few weeks to last a very long while."

"What about Aunt Leah? Are you glad she's here, too?"

"Are you glad, Gracie?" John asked, attempting to avoid telling the little girl an outright lie.

"Oh, yes. Really, really glad."

"Then I'm glad that you're glad. Now wash your face and hands and put on your pajamas while I turn down the blankets on your bed, okay?"

"Okay, Daddy." As he stood upright again, she asked shyly, "Will you read a story to me?"

"I most certainly will. Any special requests?"

"You choose tonight."

Leaving Gracie to get ready for bed on her own—something she had insisted on doing now that she would be starting first grade soon—John walked slowly down the hallway to the little girl's room. It was just across from the bedroom he'd shared with Caro, and unlike most of the rest of the house, it was clean and tidy. The cherry furniture was freshly polished, there were clean linens on the canopy bed, Gracie's books, dolls and stuffed animals were neatly arranged on the built-in shelves, and her toys were stored in the hope chest that matched the bed, dresser and nightstand.

Everything in the room was impeccably tasteful, everything chosen by Caro to suit a little girl as she grew into young womanhood. A transition Caro would have delighted in overseeing, but now never would, thanks to him.

Willing away that particularly unprofitable train of thought, John crossed to one of the two windows facing out over the front lawn, meaning to close the wide-slatted blinds. He saw that Leah had turned on the porch light, and at the edge of its glow, he saw her opening the trunk of her car, then reaching for a suitcase.

In the years they'd been apart, he'd forgotten how truly lovely she was with her dark hair falling softly against her shoulders, her green eyes flashing with intelligence. Her tall, slender body, once girlish, was now womanly in intriguing ways. She still seemed to have her own brand of inner beauty, as well—a steadfast heart that complemented the serenity of her soul.

Too bad he hadn't valued all that she was when he might have been worthy of her attention. Now…

Now John hoped she didn't plan to make herself too comfortable in his house, especially since she wasn't going to be staying long. There were too many things he'd rather she not know about him, things he would have much too hard a time hiding from her if he allowed her into his life again on a regular basis.

He was more than capable of taking care of Gracie

on his own. He'd have to pull himself together of course, but it was time he finally made the effort. The alternative—having Leah around for the next three months, a constant reminder of the lie he'd been living and would continue to live—was just the spur he needed.

"Daddy, you didn't turn on the lamp," Gracie chided gently as she joined him in her bedroom.

"I didn't expect you to be ready for a story so soon." With a flick of his wrist, John closed one set of blinds, crossed to the other window and closed the second set, then faced his daughter with a teasing smile. "Are you sure you gave your face and hands a really good wash?"

"A really, really good wash." She smiled back at him as she turned on the nightstand lamp, then hoisted herself onto the bed. "I even put my clothes in the hamper. I brushed my teeth *and* my hair, too."

"Need help with the brace?" he asked, striving for a casual tone.

"No, I can do it myself," she replied as she worked at releasing the first of several Velcro straps that held the brace firmly in place around her left leg.

"Then I guess I'd better get busy and choose a story."

Gracie had been good about wearing the ungainly brace, or at least she'd put up a good front in her own matter-of-fact way. She'd also worked hard during the daily, then weekly physical-therapy sessions following the surgery to mend the broken bones and torn ligaments, and she'd been rightfully proud of every small achievement she'd made.

She had been able to walk on her own in the bulky, metal contraption for a couple of months now. And according to the orthopedic surgeon's most recent prognosis, she would soon be able to dispense with the brace altogether.

Gracie had also worked toward accepting the finality of her mother's death, aided by a skilled psychologist and her loving grandparents. Slowly but steadily, she was returning to the happy, healthy and adventurous little girl she'd been a year ago.

John wished he could say that he'd had a hand in her recovery, but in truth, he had been too busy wallowing in his own brand of self-pity—one laced with self-contempt—to be of much help to anyone, even his beloved little girl. No more, though, he promised himself. The time had come for him to get past the anger, bitterness and pain and try to be the kind of father Gracie deserved.

Time, too, he acknowledged, to try to forget the words Caro had spoken to him those last moments they'd spent together, and what he had done to make her say them. Those awful memories only reinforced the cycle of unhealthy emotions that couldn't change the past, but had already come much too close to destroying his future.

"How about *Goodnight, Little Bear*," Gracie prompted softly, reminding John of why he stood in front of the bookcase that filled one entire wall of her room.

"An excellent choice," he said as he reached for the slender volume. "I can read another one, as well, unless you're feeling too sleepy."

"Too sleepy tonight, Daddy."

"Then it's *Goodnight, Little Bear* and good night, little Gracie. How does that sound?"

"Oh, Daddy, you're so silly sometimes." Snuggling into her pillow, she giggled as he stretched out beside her atop the pretty, pink-and-white patchwork quilt.

"Sorry, I meant to be serious," he teased, opening the book. "Guess I'd better use my growly voice again."

"Oh, no, don't do that. I don't like your growly voice at all."

"Then I'll lock it up in a box."

"And throw away the key?"

"Well, I might need the growly voice again sometime. I might have to use it with other people."

"But not with me, right, Daddy?"

"Right, Gracie, not ever with you."

"Not with Aunt Leah, either," she instructed, then yawned and closed her eyes.

John said nothing for several seconds, unable to lie to the little girl in any way. More than likely, he would have to use his growly voice and then some to get Leah Hayes out of his house. But he'd make sure Gracie wasn't within hearing distance when he did. In fact, he had every intention of dealing with Ms. Hayes just as soon as Gracie was asleep.

"Hey, are you sure you're going to be able to stay awake for even one story?" he asked, putting his arm around his daughter's shoulders and giving her a quick hug.

"Mm, yes, I can stay awake."

"Okay, then…"

Focusing on the words of the story, words he practically knew by heart after reading the book to Gracie so often, John set aside all other thoughts. Content just to be in the present moment—at home with the little girl he loved more than he could say—he began to read.

In one hand, Leah carried the suitcase that held items she'd need most her first night in John's house, in the other, Gracie's bag filled with the clothes, books and a favorite stuffed animal she'd taken to her grandparents'. Trudging back up the brick walkway, she saw a light go on above her, shining through two of the front-facing windows and adding to the glow of the porch light.

Gracie's room, she thought. John was probably putting his daughter to bed. By the time she had dumped the suitcases and taken a few minutes to freshen up in the bathroom, her niece should be tucked away for the night, perhaps already asleep. There was no reason she couldn't get a few things straightened out with John then, except her own dread of squaring off with him. It wasn't a happy prospect, by any stretch of the imagination, but an immediate, top-of-the-list must-do nonetheless.

Once inside the main entryway, Leah dropped Gracie's bag at the foot of the staircase, then, turning on lights as she went, proceeded in the direction of the room she'd be using during her stay.

The formal living and dining rooms, one opening onto either side of the entryway, obviously hadn't been used in a long time. Nor had they been cleaned recently. Dust clung to the furniture and balled up in the corners of the polished oak floors, and a cobweb hung among the crystals on the chandelier over the dining-room table. Not that bad, though, when compared to the mess she found in the kitchen and den.

Her bewilderment quickly turning to dismay, Leah halted in the center of what could have been a very cozy kitchen. With a delicate shudder, she gazed at the stacks of unwashed dishes on the countertops and in the sink and grimaced at the empty pizza boxes and Chinese-food containers piled high in the trash bin. Books and papers were scattered over the kitchen table, much as they were over the coffee table and end tables in the den.

Needless to say, this slovenliness—and that was putting it kindly—had to have been one of the reasons her father and stepmother had asked for her help. Dealing with the disarray in other people's lives—usually emotional, but occasionally physical, as well—then fading quietly into the background had become something of a specialty for her the past couple of years, she acknowledged. Longer than that, counting the lonely days she'd looked after her father following her mother's death, and the times she's sat without speaking while John poured out his heart during his parents' bitter divorce.

Then her father had met Georgette, and knowing her help was no longer needed, Leah had willingly stepped to the sidelines. She'd done the same when she realized it was Caro that John loved enough to marry. And she would do the same once more when her father and stepmother returned at the end of summer and could again keep a watchful eye on Gracie.

But August was a long way off, and she had work to do in the meantime, Leah reminded herself as she continued on to the room off the den that she assumed would be hers during her stay there.

She'd thought she'd seen the worst possible mess in the kitchen and den, but the so-called nanny's room, a fair-size bedsitting room with its own private bath, had even more horrors to offer. The bed had been left with sheets, blankets and pillows in disarray, as if the prior occupant had tumbled out, packed her bags and gone. Empty drawers gaped open in the chest and dresser, and in the bathroom used towels hung stiff as boards on the racks.

"What has been going on around here?" Leah demanded angrily of no one in particular, then answered with a twinge of sarcasm, "Apparently not much in the way of housekeeping."

Dropping her suitcase on the serviceable gray carpet, she noted that it, at least, appeared to be clean.

In the bathroom, she opened cabinet doors until she found a stack of clean towels, then washed her face and hands. Feeling a little better, she retraced her steps to the staircase, grabbed Gracie's bag and headed upstairs to the little girl's bedroom.

On the landing, Leah saw that the first two rooms on either side of the hallway stood with doors closed. The room facing the back of the house was John's study, she recalled from the photographs Caro had sent her, while the other was a guest room Caro had used mainly for storage. Farther along, two more rooms stood with doors open—the master bedroom and Gracie's room, from which the faint illumination of a night-light glowed.

Postponing her confrontation with John just a little longer, Leah walked down the hallway and peeked into her niece's bedroom. With her blond curls tumbled on the lace-edged pillow and her long eyelashes dark against her pale skin, Gracie looked like a princess peacefully sleeping under the canopy of her bed.

Leah set the bag on the floor, then tiptoed across the room. But as if sensing her aunt's presence, Gracie stirred, opened her eyes and smiled sleepily.

"I didn't mean to wake you," Leah said, sitting on the bed beside her.

"You didn't," Gracie replied. "I was waiting for you to come and say good-night."

"Well, then, good night, Gracie." Leah smiled as she gently stroked the little girl's curls, then bent to kiss her cheek.

"Good night, Aunt Leah."

"Sleep tight…"

"…and don't let the bedbugs bite," Gracie finished

with a giggle. Then, her sweet smile fading, she added more seriously, "I had a little talk with my dad."

"Oh, you did, did you?"

"He promised not to be growly anymore."

"Well, that's nice to know."

"I thought so, too." Gracie closed her eyes again and snuggled more deeply under the quilt. "See you in the morning?" she asked softly.

"Count on it," Leah said as she tucked the covers around the little girl's shoulders.

She might not have had a warm welcome from John, much less a clean bed in which to sleep, but she wasn't going to desert her niece under any circumstances.

Out in the hallway again, Leah paused. She was tempted to go back downstairs and set to work making her room habitable for the night. It was a perfectly good excuse to put off talking to John until the following day. But she knew that the sooner she faced him, the better it would be for all concerned.

She didn't want him thinking she was going to creep around his house, giving him a wide berth and staying out of his way like a frightened puppy. She'd stood up to him often enough in the past without any serious repercussions. Granted, they had been children rather than adults then, but surely their maturity would work in her favor now. After all, he'd promised Gracie he wouldn't be growly anymore, she told herself with a slight smile. She hoped the promise had included conversations with her, as well as his daughter.

Leah rapped firmly on the door to John's study. Then, throwing caution to the wind, she walked in without waiting for an invitation. The room was as dark as the rest of the house had been. Only a glimmer of outside light coming through the blinds at the windows delineated the placement of the furnishings—a large desk and chair, bookshelves, a small leather sofa. Surprisingly well ordered, she noted, considering the condition of the rest of the house.

John stood by one of the windows, his back to her, making no effort to acknowledge her presence. Hands in the pockets of his jeans, his shoulders slumped, he gazed out at only he knew what.

Leah had been determined to stand up to him, to speak her mind about his earlier behavior and lay some ground rules. But the sight of him looking so…forlorn stole away the words she'd been prepared to say. Instead, she moved toward him quietly, wanting only to put her arms around him, to hold him close and assure him that everything would be all right.

Yes, his beloved Caro was dead, but he had Gracie to consider. And now *she* was there—his once and always friend—to help him begin to heal.

"Get out of here, Leah."

Though pitched low, John's voice lashed like a whip across the room, halting her in midstep. Momentarily stunned by the depth of his animosity toward her, Leah gripped the edge of his desk to steady herself. She saw in an instant how his shoulders had straightened, how he now held his hands at his sides, clenched into fists.

He was ready for a fight. More than that, he wanted one. But why? she wondered. She'd never been his enemy—

"Are you deaf, Leah? I told you to get out," he repeated, this time honoring her with a pointed glance over one shoulder.

"John, please, I've come here to help," she began, trying to get him to be reasonable.

"I don't want or need your charity," he muttered darkly, turning away again.

"I'm not sure what you mean by charity." Truly puzzled by his comment, she eyed him silently, waiting for some further explanation. When he offered none, she ventured softly, "You obviously need some help around here and I'm more than willing to provide it. I thought you understood. More than that, I thought you agreed—"

"Me, agree? Not likely, Leah. And as for you being willing?" He laughed softly without any humor. "You're only here because Cameron and Georgette played on your sympathy."

"How can you say that?" she demanded, unable to hide her dismay. "Surely you know how much I care about you and Gracie."

Her father and stepmother *had* played on her sympathy, but John had to know that that alone wouldn't have brought her home again. Why, then, was he treating her like an adversary?

"Right, Leah. You care about us so much that you've only now come back to Missoula after eight years away. You didn't even bother to come home for Caro's funeral." He paused for a moment, as if only then aware of what he'd revealed, then forged on with surly determination. "Now you want me to believe you're here out of the goodness of your heart and you expect me to be grateful? No way in hell—"

"I was traveling in Southeast Asia when Caro died. I didn't even know about the accident until two weeks after it happened," Leah reminded him, realizing at last what had caused him to be so upset with her. She'd thought he knew and understood why she hadn't been able to be there for him during those weeks immediately following Caro's death. But it seemed he hadn't, and he'd held it against her ever since. "I wrote to you then, John. A long letter you never answered. If you needed me, why didn't you let me know? I would have come."

"Because I didn't need you then, just like I don't need you now. Simple enough, isn't it? So why don't you grab your suitcase and just get the hell out of here," he said again with a quiet emphasis that almost had her scurrying to obey.

Only the realization of how deeply he'd been hurt by her absence made her stand firm. Now that she knew how badly she'd let John down after Caro died, she wasn't going to let him down again. There was Gracie to consider, too, and the awful disorder downstairs. Regardless of what he said or did, he needed her here, and here she was going to stay.

"I'll get out of your study…for now. You're obviously in the midst of a self-indulgent wallow of some sort, and I might as well leave you to it," she stated with surprising self-possession. "But I'm not getting out of your house, not tonight or tomorrow or the day after that. Somebody needs to clean up the mess you've made downstairs before your daughter sees it. And somebody certainly needs to look after Gracie until Cameron and Georgette return in August. Since you seem too busy feeling sorry for yourself to even take out the trash, and since you've already succeeded in running off two nannies in the past nine months, you're stuck with me. Like it or not, I suggest you get used to it," she finished with a defiant tip of her chin.

"I didn't run off two nannies in nine months," he snapped back, glaring at her. "The first one left to take a higher-paying job in Seattle. I caught the second one in bed with a man in the middle of the day while Gracie was alone in her room under orders not to come out. Despite what you've obviously been told, I'm not quite the ogre I've been portrayed as being.''

"No one has portrayed you as an ogre, and I don't consider you one, either. But by the same token, I'm not the enemy here," she insisted, hoping to mollify him enough that he would give her at least a little cooperation.

"You did say you'd get out of my study, didn't you?" he asked almost conversationally, obviously choosing to ignore her attempt to soften his mood. "Anytime now would be good for me."

Both angered and exasperated by his callous dismissal but trying hard not to show it, Leah spun on her heel and crossed to the doorway, then paused.

"I never knew you could be such a jerk, John Bennett," she tossed back at him, unable to keep the hurt she was feeling from echoing in her voice.

"There's a lot you don't know about me, Leah," he warned softly, turning to face her fully for the first time since she'd entered his study. "A lot you don't want to know, believe me."

There was a new element in his tone, a self-loathing that caught Leah completely by surprise. But she was too caught up in her anger with him to do more than file the thought away for future consideration.

"Right now I'd have to agree with you," she shot back.

Her head held high, Leah quietly left and closed the door behind her. She paused in the hallway to take a deep, calming breath, then suddenly realized that Gracie could have overheard their every word. With a sense of dread, she hurried down the hallway, then sighed with relief. A glance in the little girl's bedroom assured her that Gracie was sleeping soundly.

While Leah had no intention of allowing John to treat her badly, she didn't want his daughter witnessing the kind of exchange they'd just had. She didn't think John would, either, but she couldn't be absolutely sure. His emotions seemed much too volatile.

She could only hope that in the days ahead the diplomacy she'd developed dealing with the more overbearing parents she'd come up against as a teacher would work to her advantage with him, as well.

Obviously John was still grieving deeply for Caro. That alone gave her good reason to make allowances for his behavior. And although he hadn't said as much in so many words, he'd also been hurt by *her* absence after Caro's death.

Leah had thought about coming home many times in the months since the accident, but she'd always found excuses to stay away. Not because she hadn't cared about John, she admitted. In fact, she'd cared about him too much and hadn't wanted him to know it.

During all the years John had been married to Caro, Leah had never really stopped loving him. Selfishly, she had sought to avoid the one situation guaranteed to cause her heartache, and in the process she had lost what friendship they'd once shared.

Well, so be it, she thought as she headed downstairs to strip the linens from the bed in her room and put them in the washing machine. It wasn't necessary for them to be friends for her to take care of Gracie. Nor was their friendship necessary for her to scrub pots and pans, carry out the trash, load the dishwasher and wipe down countertops, she added as she surveyed the kitchen with her hands on her hips.

But it would have been so much easier being there with John if she could have counted on him treating her kindly. She deserved at least that much from him without having to demand it. She still hadn't given up completely, at least not yet. He couldn't ignore indefinitely the past they'd shared. He might try, but she wasn't going to let him.

Eventually, he would realize she was there for his benefit as well as Gracie's. All she had to do was be patient, and she had gotten very good at that over the years, she thought, as she grimly set to work filling the sink with hot, soapy water to soak the crusty pots and pans left on the stove.

Chapter Three

They were at it again, John thought, eyeing the clock on his nightstand with bleary eyes. Not quite seven in the morning, and for the third day in a row, the sound of feminine voices—light, bright and much too cheerful, at least to his way of thinking—drifted into his bedroom from the kitchen directly below.

He had never been an early riser, nor had Caro. But Leah and Gracie seemed to delight in waking up with the birds, then waking him up, as well, with their airy chatter, the bang of pots and pans, and the scent of breakfast cooking.

With a low groan, John sat up and scrubbed his hands through his shaggy hair. Somehow, in the days since her arrival Sunday night, Leah had quietly and efficiently taken over responsibility for his home, as well as his daughter. Not that he'd put up much of a fight. He hadn't yet stayed in the house with Leah long enough for that to happen.

Monday morning he had gone downstairs, totally uncertain of his reception. His behavior toward Leah the night before had been abominable, but he had no intention of apologizing to her. He didn't want or need her in his home, and any nicety on his part would only make it that much harder to get rid of her, as he kept telling himself he had every intention of doing very soon.

Shifting in his bed, he remembered how he'd walked into the spotlessly clean kitchen that first morning to find Leah and Gracie at the table, empty plates pushed aside, their heads bent over the comics in the daily paper.

"Daddy?" Gracie had looked up at him with a surprised smile. "You got up early today."

"Couldn't sleep with all the racket down here," he'd replied, not sounding nearly as gruff as he should have under the circumstances.

Leah, too, had acknowledged his presence, but her smile hadn't quite erased the wary look in her eyes.

"There's bacon in the oven," she'd said. "It won't take me long to scramble a couple of eggs for you if you're hungry, or I can put some bread in the toaster...."

"Thanks, but I'll just have coffee." He'd filled the thermal mug he used, then dug in a drawer for paper and pen. "Here's the telephone number for my office at the university. I'll be there all day if you need me. Don't bother to wait dinner." He'd set the note on the table, then added by way of explanation when he'd seen the crestfallen look on Gracie's face, "I have a meeting with the dean that I've put off for a couple of weeks already. There's no getting out of it today."

"Can we come see you at your office?" Gracie had asked, her voice filled with hope.

"Maybe another day," he'd replied, then hesitated, not really as anxious to get away as he'd been initially.

"We have to go to the grocery store this morning, Gracie, and we haven't even begun to put together our list yet," Leah reminded the little girl gently.

"Oh, yeah, you'll need some money."

John had frowned as he dug in his back pocket for his wallet, afraid that he didn't have enough cash on hand to cover all the things he imagined Leah would probably have to buy. He had gotten in the habit of keeping only a minimal amount of perishable food in the house.

"I've got it covered. Pay me back when you can," she'd told him.

"Right, I will."

He'd left then, the memory of the reproach he'd seen in Leah's eyes staying with him not only all day, but also well into the night. He hadn't been so busy that he'd had to go to the university quite so early that day, and he could have come home much sooner than he had, as well. Instead, he'd waited purposely until he'd been sure that Leah and Gracie had both gone to bed.

Tuesday morning had been a replay of Monday morning except that Leah's homemaking efforts on Monday had made him feel even guiltier. Not only had there been leftover meat loaf in the refrigerator, but a chocolate layer cake on the counter. And the rest of the house, now as immaculate as the kitchen, had smelled of fresh air and lemon oil.

Instead of being duly contrite, though, he had allowed his irritation at himself to show and be misconstrued.

"I appreciate your efforts, Leah, but you don't have to clean my house," he'd said as he'd filled his mug at the counter. "I can hire a maid service to come in once a week."

"But it was fun, Daddy," Gracie had said. "Leah let me push the vacuum cleaner and spray the furniture polish on the tables. I helped her bake a cake, too, and we made cinnamon rolls for breakfast today. Wait'll you taste them. They are so, so yummy."

There had been a wary look in Leah's lovely eyes again when he'd turned to meet her gaze. But there had been the barest hint of anger, as well, and it had echoed in her voice when she spoke.

"There's no need to hire a maid service while I'm here, John," she said. "I intend to earn my keep, you know. By the way, the receipt for the groceries I bought is on the windowsill. You can give me a check to cover the cost whenever you have a chance. Gracie requested spaghetti for dinner tonight, too, hoping you'd eat with us."

"Sorry, I can't be here," he'd answered curtly, then had wanted to kick himself when he'd seen Gracie duck her head to hide her disappointment.

"You're awfully busy for June, aren't you?" Leah had asked, politely yet pointedly.

"I've just gotten funding for an important research project," he'd answered, his tone more defensive than he'd intended. "I'd like to have it well under way before classes start again in the fall."

"I see," she'd said, her own tone making it evident that she didn't really. Then she'd added with a killer smile that had made his breath catch, "Good thing I'm here, then, isn't it?"

"I think so," Gracie had said, reminding John of her presence. "Don't you, Daddy?"

"Yes, of course. What would we do without your aunt

Leah?'' He'd allowed just enough sarcasm into his tone to wipe the smile off Leah's face without upsetting Gracie, something he'd learned to do years ago with Caro.

He'd headed out again after that, feeling every bit the jerk Leah had accused him of being Sunday night. To make bad matters worse, his rude behavior toward her wasn't even doing him any good. She was too strong-minded and stubborn to let him run her off.

In fact, he'd realized as he'd stood at the kitchen counter just after midnight eating cold spaghetti that he was making his own life more difficult—not to mention more miserable—by going to such great lengths to avoid Leah's company. She'd put him on notice that she intended to dig in her heels for the duration of the summer, and what was so bad about that?

Nothing, he acknowledged as he got out of bed now. She'd made his home a clean and comfortable place to be again, although wisely she hadn't gone into his study or his bedroom yet. He was the one staying away by choice simply because he didn't want to admit to her, or to himself, how glad he was that she was there.

That would mean apologizing for his rudeness the night she'd arrived, and that, in turn, might very well lead her to expect further explanations he had no intention of giving. There were things about himself and Caro and their life together, especially during the last few months of their marriage, that he didn't want Leah to ever know.

Showered and dressed, John headed downstairs, intending to go to his office at the university as he had the past couple of days. He was surprised to find neither Leah nor Gracie in the kitchen, though a fresh pot of coffee and his mug sat on the counter, along with a box of cereal, a bowl and a spoon.

Puzzled by Leah and Gracie's absence, he reached for the coffeepot. Through the window over the sink, he glimpsed a flash of red, then froze, hand in the air just shy of the pot's handle. Leah was dressed in a pair of faded denim shorts, very *short* shorts that showed off her long legs to advantage, and a red tank top under which she wore—from the way her full, firm breasts pushed against the fabric—nothing at all.

Looking about sixteen with her hair pulled back in a saucy ponytail, she was bent over the lawn mower, fiddling with the choke. Gracie, standing safely off to one side, chattered happily, apparently asking questions that Leah answered in ways that made the little girl giggle with delight.

Without really thinking, John moved to the kitchen door, pulled it open and strode out onto the patio.

"What do you think you're doing?" he asked, making no effort to hide his exasperation.

"Mowing the grass," Leah replied in a mild tone, glancing back at him for an instant before she unscrewed the cap on the mower's fuel tank. "Unless I have to go to the service station to buy a couple of gallons of gas. *Then* I'll be mowing the grass."

"And we're going to weed the flower beds, too," Gracie declared. "Maybe, if we have time, we're going to the nursery to buy some plants, too. We both like roses best, you know."

No, he hadn't known that about either Gracie or Leah, John ruefully admitted to himself.

"I was going to mow the lawn," he said. The yard wasn't that overgrown yet, was it? Well, yes, he realized after a swift survey, it was.

Leah shot him a skeptical look as she straightened.

"When, exactly?" she asked casually, wiping her hands on the seat of her shorts.

"Eventually," he muttered, shifting from one foot to the other uncomfortably as he looked away from her penetrating gaze.

"We have to do it today, Daddy, 'cause everybody's mad at us," Gracie stated in a solemn tone. "Mrs. Thomason and Mr. Carey and the Donovans—both of them."

"Mad at us?" He eyed first Gracie, then Leah in confusion.

"Apparently your neighbors, at least the ones Gracie mentioned, seem to feel property values on the street are set to take a nosedive if we don't get your yard cleaned up within the next twenty-four hours," Leah explained with an all-too-sweet smile.

"How do you know that?" John demanded.

"They each took the opportunity to tell me personally. And I assured them all, personally, that I'd see it was taken care of immediately."

"You're not mowing the lawn, Leah."

"But, Daddy, we have to," Gracie insisted.

"No, I have to, and I will just as soon as I change my clothes," he assured his daughter.

"What about your research project?" Leah reminded him in a tone he couldn't quite read.

"I have teaching assistants working on it, too."

"Will wonders never cease? Teaching assistants. However did you manage to conjure them up just now?"

"Do I need to buy gas for the mower or is the tank full?" John asked, choosing to ignore her teasing words and her equally teasing smile despite the shaft of warmth the two combined sent straight to his heart.

He wasn't going to be able to use his work as an

excuse to stay away anymore, and she knew it. But it wouldn't be wise to encourage her gloating. She might be tempted to try to get him to lower his guard even more, and that he couldn't afford to do around her. He'd only end up telling her things about himself he'd really rather not.

"Looked to me like the tank's full," she advised. Then to Gracie she added, "Come on, sweetie, let's get started on the front flower bed, okay?"

"We'll definitely have time to buy some roses now, won't we?" Gracie asked as she and Leah collected the gardening tools already laid out on the patio table.

"If not today, tomorrow for sure," Leah replied.

"You'll go with us, too, won't you, Daddy?"

John hesitated, trying to come up with a reason besides work to say no. But the hopeful look on Gracie's face, combined with the warning flash in Leah's eyes, had him saying, instead, "Yeah, sure, I'll go to the nursery with you. Can't have you two buying out the place on me like you did when you went grocery shopping without me."

"He's actually more worried about all the planting he might have to do later," Leah said sagely.

"But we'll help him, won't we?"

"We'll help him all he wants," Leah said, and the look she gave him before she turned away conveyed much more than what her words alone implied.

Watching as Leah and Gracie disappeared around the side of the house, John allowed himself to consider all the ways he could have used Leah's help but wouldn't. And he was reminded yet again of how much he'd missed her in all the years she'd been away. She had always been good for his soul; she could be again.

But he couldn't attempt to rekindle the relationship

they'd shared in years past for so many reasons, chief among them that friendship would no longer be enough for him. And intimacy—the kind of ardent sexual intimacy he could easily imagine having with her—demanded an honesty he could never allow himself to express.

Leah tried not to feel too smug about the slight inroad she'd made into John's icy reserve of the past few days. She hadn't intended to embarrass him into helping with the yard work. She'd been fully prepared to mow and rake and weed flower beds with Gracie's limited help. But given the opportunity to draw John into an activity involving his daughter, she'd have been a fool not to take it.

Her only real hope of making the summer a success for Gracie was to engage John's cooperation. And as long as he kept running off to his office at the university, she hadn't any hope of doing that. She wanted him to spend time with his daughter, too, and had begun to fear that her constant presence was the main reason he didn't.

Leah could see how much he loved Gracie, yet she also sensed a puzzling restraint in him toward the little girl. Had the pain of losing Caro been so great that he was now afraid to let himself acknowledge his love for anyone else, including his own daughter? Leah hoped not. Gracie needed him, not at a benevolent distance, but up close and personal, with his deepest emotions fully and completely committed.

"All done here?"

John's gruff, matter-of-fact voice startled Leah so much that she lost her grip on the flat of pink-and-white petunias she and Gracie had chosen from the rows on display at the nursery. Instinctively John reached around her with both arms and helped her catch it before it hit the ground. His muscular chest pressed against her back, his strong, broad hands covering hers, he stood for several exquisitely long moments, seeming to hold his breath just as she did.

Leah wanted to lean into him and savor the warmth of his body, wanted to tip back her head and smile up at him teasingly as she would have in the past. Instead, she stood as if frozen in place, her heart thudding slowly in her chest, waiting for whatever angry recrimination he would no doubt choose to hurtle her way.

"Aunt Leah, you almost dropped our petunias," Gracie said, then added with a giggle, "Good thing Daddy was here."

"A very good thing," Leah agreed, sending the little girl a grateful smile.

"I didn't mean to scare you," John said as he finally eased away from her.

"My fault for not paying attention."

"Well, pay attention to this," he said in an almost teasing tone that put Leah in mind of years past. "That is the last flat of flowers going on our tab today, unless one of you wants to walk home. The Jeep is now holding all the plants it can hold and still have room to spare for the three of us. Don't forget we're going to have to plant all that stuff, too."

"I know, Daddy, and I'm gonna help. But we want to stop for burgers and fries first, don't we, Aunt Leah?"

"Trying to take advantage of my good mood, huh?"

"You're in a good mood today?" Leah couldn't help but quip as they waited for John to pay for the plants they'd chosen.

John eyed her quizzically for several seconds, apparently giving her question serious consideration.

"Yes," he admitted at last, a hint of surprise in his voice. "I am."

"Must be something in the air," she offered lightly.

"Or maybe the company I'm keeping." He held her gaze an instant longer, then scooped Gracie into his arms. "Yeah, it has to be this lovely little girl's company."

"Oh, Daddy, you're so funny sometimes."

He had meant Gracie of course, Leah told herself as they piled into the Jeep and headed for her niece's favorite fast-food restaurant. But that didn't stop her heart from beating faster.

Back at the house again, there was a message waiting for John on the answering machine. A problem had come up at the university lab that required his immediate attention.

"So much for leaving the teaching assistants in charge," he grumbled after explaining the situation to Leah and Gracie.

"No problem," Leah told him cheerfully for Gracie's sake. "The really hard work is all done. We shouldn't have any trouble putting the plants we bought in the beds after we eat, right, sweetie?"

"Right, Aunt Leah," the little girl agreed happily enough as she peeled the wrapper off her cheeseburger.

"Don't try to move the heavier containers," John instructed, already withdrawing from their company as he headed toward the hallway.

Leah had thought, obviously in error, that he didn't really want to go to the lab.

"At least eat something first," she urged, waving a hand at the burgers and fries she'd set out on the table.

"I have to take a shower," he called over his shoulder. "I'll eat on the way to the lab."

He was back in the kitchen in fifteen minutes, wearing khaki pants and a black knit T-shirt, looking so handsome that Leah's heart ached. Then he was out the door with his food in hand, leaving them with a wave. Leah felt a sense of regret as she heard the Jeep's engine roar to life.

They had been making some fairly decent progress in the getting-to-know-each-other-again department. For the first time since she'd arrived there Sunday night, she'd felt reasonably relaxed in John's presence, and he'd seemed reasonably relaxed in hers, as well.

Would he put up the wall of resistance between them when they were next together? she wondered. Would he revert to the man she'd come to dread the past couple of days?

Not if she had anything to say about it, she vowed as she dipped a French fry into ketchup, then munched on it contentedly.

"Why are you smiling, Aunt Leah?"

"I'm thinking about how much fun we had this morning, and how lovely the yard looks now. And I'm thinking that if we get everything planted by tomorrow afternoon, we could plan to have a picnic on Friday."

"Oh, I love picnics!" Gracie said.

"Well, then, let's clean up this mess and start putting our flowers in their beds."

"Do you think my dad would like to go with us on the picnic?"

"Maybe," Leah replied, careful not to get the little girl's hopes up too high.

John has always loved going on picnics, too, and with luck, he would have the crisis at the lab under control by Friday. After the way he'd behaved today, she wanted to believe he'd make the effort to be with them again, for Gracie's sake, if nothing else.

Having him along would be fun for her, too, Leah admitted as she and Gracie finished tidying the kitchen. He had definitely begun to mellow toward her. The more fun things she could plan for them to do together, the more likely he was to mellow even more. And that would be such a good thing...for all of them.

Chapter Four

John stood in front of the refrigerator with the door wide-open, the light from its interior the only light in the kitchen at one-thirty in the morning. Methodically he opened first one plastic container, then another as he tried to decide which of the various leftovers from the meals Leah had prepared appealed most to him. There'd been meat loaf Monday night, the spaghetti he'd already sampled Tuesday night, and tonight…ah, yes, this must be it—chicken in some kind of a cream sauce that included chunks of onion, carrot and mushrooms.

Too good to eat cold from the container, he decided, switching on the light over the stove. With a minimum of clatter, he found a plate to put in the microwave oven, transferred a hefty portion of the chicken and vegetables onto it, then stood by the counter and waited for it to heat.

Embarrassing, really, to steal around his own kitchen

in the dead of night eating leftovers when he could have sat down at the table earlier with Leah and Gracie like any sensible person. But he'd set the pattern Monday night, and he wasn't sure how to break it without seeming obvious. Though obvious about what, he didn't know.

He'd had a perfect right to join Leah and Gracie for dinner each of the preceding evenings. Not that anyone had kept him away except himself. After the time he'd spent with them that morning, he'd wanted to come home much sooner than he actually had.

He'd gotten sidetracked at the university lab, though, coping with first one unanticipated problem and then another as the afternoon wore on. He'd retreated to his office at last, when everything seemed to be under control, only to have his attention diverted again as he'd made an attempt to clear away part of the mountain of paperwork that had accumulated over the past several months.

It had been almost eight by the time he'd noticed the deepening shadows in the corners of his office and glanced at the clock on his desk to check the time. He could have left then, but all the mowing and raking he'd done earlier in the day finally seemed to have caught up with him. Suddenly he'd felt too tired to do more than stretch out on the old sofa he'd installed for just such an occasion. Just for a few minutes, he'd assured himself, only to awaken several hours later, rested and ready to eat.

The scent of Leah's chicken and vegetables wafted from the microwave oven, making John's mouth water and his stomach growl. He opened the door before the timer could beep, grabbed the plate and almost dropped it when the hot china burned his fingers. Muttering a curse, he jostled the plate from hand to hand until he could set in on the table, then he dug a knife and fork from the silverware drawer and grabbed an icy cold beer from the refrigerator.

He really had to try to get on a more reasonable schedule, he admonished himself, twisting the cap off the bottle. He'd be lucky to get back to sleep by three, and then, if their pattern continued, Leah and Gracie would be up at six, waking him, as well.

With a groan, half in pleasure at the wonderful taste of the chicken and half in anticipation of yet another bleary-eyed morning to come, John reached for his beer, tipped it back and took a long swallow, then another. A flicker of movement at the doorway to the den caught his eye, startling him.

He jerked with surprise, and the second swallow of beer went down his throat the wrong way. Eyes watering, he started to cough. Several moments passed before he managed to get his breath back. Then, as he wiped the tears from his eyes with the back of his hand, he realized he was no longer alone in the kitchen.

Leah stood in the doorway, a look of concern in her sleepy eyes. Her shiny brown hair was tousled in an enticingly touchable way, and she wore only an oversize black T-shirt with a silver lightning bolt across the front. The garment barely came to midthigh, accentuating her long, slender legs. To John, it looked sexier than any silk-and-satin nightgown might have.

First short denim shorts and a red tank top without benefit of a bra, then a black T-shirt that should have at least covered her knees. She was making him hot for her, hungry for her, in ways he couldn't afford to be. And she was doing it innocently, without any overt provocation, because she wouldn't know, couldn't know from his behavior toward her so far how swiftly her place in his heart was being restored.

Eight years ago John hadn't realized that with only the slightest shift in his awareness of Leah, his feelings for her would have quickly exceeded the normal bounds of friendship. He was older than she by several years, so he had assumed the role of her protector early on in their relationship and had taken her quiet, steady, faithful companionship not only at face value, but also for granted.

Then, just as he'd begun to realize Leah was no longer a girl, but a vibrant young woman on the verge of adulthood, Caro had come into their lives, so bright and so beautiful. He'd been dazzled by her, too dazzled to see the recklessness and irresponsibility in her nature, and the constant need to be amused, as well as amusing, that were also a part of her personality.

Even though Leah had been only eighteen, she'd actually been the one who embodied all the things he'd really needed. But imperceptive as he'd been at the time, not to mention ruled more by hormones than common sense, he'd wanted only Caro, and much to his later dismay, Caro had been the one he'd gotten.

"Hey, are you okay?" Leah asked, her soft voice filled with concern.

Instead of scurrying away as he'd thought she would, she joined him in the kitchen, obviously unaware or uncaring that she was intruding on his privacy. Considering her behavior the past few days, John would have bet on the latter. She'd toughened up quite a bit over the past eight years, his little Leah. Only, she wasn't little anymore, and she certainly wasn't his.

"I didn't mean to wake you," he said, allowing a

gruff note into his voice, hoping to chase her back
to bed.

"I made the mistake of falling asleep on the sofa earlier," she replied. "By the time I got into bed, I wasn't
really that tired anymore, so I was half-awake already
when I heard you come in."

She sauntered past him, leaving a hint of lavender
scent behind to tease him, opened the refrigerator door,
then bent over gracefully to retrieve a beer for herself.

John sat frozen in place, his gaze riveted to the display
of lacy panties her pose revealed. Only when she
straightened again was he able to look away and quickly
take several more slugs of his beer. By the time she'd
pulled out a chair and joined him at the table, he had as
much of his attention as possible focused on his plate of
food.

"There's some rice to go with the chicken if you want
it," she said. "I can get it for you. It's in another container."

"No, thanks. This is fine," he hastened to assure her,
not trusting what he might be tempted to do if he had
to watch her bend over in front of the refrigerator again.

He ate another mouthful of chicken while she sipped
her beer, then shot a glance her way and saw that she
was watching him, not only openly, but intently. Though
she was fully awake now, she still looked ready to be
dragged back to bed. Feeling the heat rise in his cheeks,
he looked down at his plate again.

He had never once thought of taking Leah to bed in
the past. Well, he had a few times in the months just
before he'd lost what wits he had over Caro. But he'd
never let Leah know it, either by word or deed. And that
had been years ago.

Even if he could justify initiating a sexual relationship

after such a long time, he wasn't foolish enough to think she'd agree to it. For one thing, her life was in Chicago, and for another, there surely had to be someone special with whom she shared that life—though John couldn't imagine any man allowing Leah to go off to Montana for an entire summer without pitching a fit.

"Are you sure?" she asked, interrupting his train of thought.

"About what?" he shot back, afraid he'd missed something important she might have said.

"The chicken."

"Oh, yeah, it's fine, just like I said. More than fine. It's really very, very good. Why?"

"You had a funny look on your face, that's all," she replied.

"It had nothing to do with the chicken or anything else important," he assured her, desperate to ward off any further questions concerning his current state of mind. "You're really quite an excellent cook, Leah."

"I like to experiment in the kitchen." She gave an offhand shrug, then added, "It would have tasted even better if you'd joined us for dinner, though. That particular dish is always best hot out of the oven. You do know you're welcome to join us, don't you?"

"Yes, of course. It *is* my house." Again he used an unnecessarily gruff tone of voice, but again, Leah didn't appear even the slightest bit fazed by it.

"Thanks for all your help with the yard work today, too. It meant a lot to Gracie having you here, and to me," she acknowledged lightly, adding the last almost as an afterthought. "I don't mind weeding beds and planting flowers, but I truly hate pushing a lawn mower."

"But you would have done it, wouldn't you."

"If I'd had to, yes. Anything to keep from being way-laid by another of your neighbors." She smiled slightly, then added, "You know, John, they've been concerned about you. I mean you, personally, not just the condition of your yard."

"I can't imagine why. I'm fine."

He picked up his empty plate and stood, anxious to avoid any further discussion of what he considered his personal business. He wasn't about to open that door to Leah. Revelations might spill out that wouldn't do either of them any good.

"You bury yourself in your work at the university, you spend hardly any time at all with a daughter who loves you and needs you, you treat me like an enemy when we were once the best of friends..." She stopped to take a breath.

"Not tonight, Leah. Don't start on me tonight," he said, more tired than angry as he set his plate in the sink, then braced his hands on the counter, his back to her.

He felt the warm, gentle, tentative and totally unex-pected touch of her hand on his shoulder at the same instant her voice sounded right behind him. "John, please don't keep pushing me away. I can only imagine the pain you've suffered since Caro's death. I've grieved for her, too, and I always will. But surely you know that she wouldn't have wanted you to stop living yourself just because she's gone. Caro wasn't like that. Caro would have expected you to put the pieces of your life back together again, not only for your sake, but for Gra-cie's. Caro would have wanted—"

Unable to contain himself any longer, John spun around and grabbed Leah by her upper arms. His intent had been to give her a good shake just to shut her up, but as he towered over her, he made the mistake of meeting her gaze. The vulnerability in her wide, green eyes cut through him like a knife, slicing away the protective layer of anger and frustration inside him and laying bare a longing so deep and so complete it sent a tremor through his body.

His grip on her arms loosened, and his hands slid up to her shoulders. He began to pull her closer, and she came willingly at his urging, resting her hands on his chest. Then the realization of what he was about to do hit him like a wave of icy water, dousing completely the newly kindled flame of his desire.

"You have no idea what Caro wanted, Leah, no idea at all," he growled, the sudden sense of overwhelming weariness that gripped him echoing in his voice. "And any pain I've suffered since her death I've deserved. Not that it's your business one way or another. As for Gracie, I admit I haven't been available for her the way I should have over the past few months. But I'm more than able, not to mention more than willing, to take care of her on my own now."

"Then maybe I should leave," Leah said softly. "Especially if you're staying away from the house because I'm here."

For one long moment John couldn't quite believe he'd heard her right. Instead of snapping back at him angrily or prodding him patiently for an explanation as he'd fully expected she would, she had calmly, quietly, given in to what he wanted. Only it wasn't what he wanted, not really.

He had Gracie's well-being to take into consideration, too. Having Leah in their home had been so obviously good for the little girl. That alone was enough to negate any annoyance, large or small, Leah caused him personally.

Yeah, sure, she was annoying the hell out of him, John thought, still looking into her eyes, still savoring the warmth of her hands resting delicately on his chest. Next thing he knew, he'd be telling himself he didn't want to pull her into an embrace and kiss her senseless—

Letting go of Leah as suddenly as he'd grabbed her, John brushed past her and strode purposefully across the kitchen toward the doorway to the front hall.

"There's no need for you to leave unless you want to," he said. "Gracie likes having you here, and as long as she's happy with the arrangement, then so am I."

"My sentiments exactly," Leah replied, the barest hint of anger in her tone.

It was almost as if she knew instinctively that he wanted her there with them, as well, and considered him a coward for not saying so. Or maybe he was just projecting his own thoughts regarding his faintheartedness onto her.

"Then we're in agreement that you'll stay for the summer?" He paused in the doorway and glanced back at her, aware that he was holding his breath as he waited for her to answer him.

"Only if you start spending more time with Gracie. You do have teaching assistants to help with your project at the university lab, and you are entitled to some vacation time."

"I am planning on being more available," he said.

"Then, yes, we're in agreement. I'll stay for the summer."

"Fine," he muttered, and with a curt nod that totally belied the sense of relief zinging through him, John turned away again. He walked slowly through the dark house to the staircase, then up to his bedroom, stopping first to check on Gracie.

Snuggled cozily under her quilt, the little girl was sound asleep. Standing just inside her bedroom doorway, he gazed at her with the same sense of wonder and joy that she'd stirred in him the day she'd been born. How happy he'd been then to welcome this child into his life, and how happy he would always be to have her as his precious daughter. Despite the bitter, angry words Caro had hurled at him the night she died, that would never change.

His marriage might have been a lie, his family not really, truly his in the way he'd believed it to be, but he loved Gracie no less. She was the light of his life.

Gracie was also the one who'd brought Leah back into his life. And the one who would keep her there at least a little while longer, and for that, John was more grateful than he could say.

Chapter Five

"What time do you girls usually eat dinner?" John asked.

"Five-thirty or sometimes six o'clock," Gracie replied, then grinned at her father as she added excitedly, "Why, Daddy? Are you going to be home in time to eat with us tonight?"

Leah smiled, too, as she watched John fill his coffee mug at the counter. She sat at the table with Gracie, the morning paper spread out in front of her, though she hadn't grasped much of what she'd been trying to read even before John joined them in the kitchen. Her mind kept drifting back to a much earlier hour of the morning when she'd come upon him here and the conversation they'd had.

Oh, right, it had been the *conversation* she'd had on her mind. She hadn't thought once about the way he'd held her by the arms, the way his grip had turned into a caress as his hands moved to her shoulders, the way he'd met her eyes, a new and unmistakable awareness in the pale gray depths of his just before he'd stalked off—

"I should be, if that's okay with you."

His glance over one shoulder was directed at Leah, and she acknowledged it, her smile widening.

"That would be great, wouldn't it, Gracie?"

"Oh, yes! You can help us make the pizza, Daddy."

"We can order pizza," John began, then apparently caight the subtle shake of Leah's head. "But making our own sounds like a lot of fun."

"I thought so, too," Leah said. "Gracie suggested it, and sometimes she has the best ideas."

"We won't start till you get here, okay, Daddy?"

"Okay, Gracie."

"So don't be late."

"I won't, sweetie."

He crossed to the table and dropped a kiss on his daughter's blond, curly hair. For just an instant, as she watched them together, Leah imagined how she would feel if John kissed her goodbye, as well—not on the top of her head, but smack on her mouth.

Wonderful, she decided; it would feel just wonderful.

"What do you two have planned for the day?" John asked Leah as he returned to the counter to collect his mug.

"We're going to finish planting the flowers we bought," Leah replied, tantalized by the faint spicy scent of his aftershave.

"There were quite a few, weren't there." He offered her a teasing smile that reminded her of years past, then crossed to the outside door and reached for the knob.

Warmed by his easy banter, unexpected as it was, Leah shot him a wry look. "I would say we went a bit overboard at the nursery yesterday, but then somebody might say he told me so.''

''Told you so,'' John said, all but hooting with satisfaction, and was gone.

''Do you really think he'll come home for dinner tonight?'' Gracie asked, sounding doubtful after the door closed behind him. ''He could get real busy and have to work late again and forget to tell us.''

''He'll be here, Gracie,'' Leah assured the little girl, thinking he would be even if it meant she had to track him down at the university and drag him home personally.

''But sometimes he forgets.''

''Then we'll give him a call at four o'clock and remind him to come home. How does that sound to you?''

''That sounds like a plan, man,'' Gracie answered, giggling with delight at the rhyme she'd made.

''You're silly sometimes, you know?''

''You, too, Aunt Leah.''

''I do my best.'' She reached out and ruffled Gracie's curls, then pushed away from the table. ''Let's clean up the kitchen first, then it's planting time again.''

''Can I rinse the dishes and put them in the dishwasher?''

''Sure thing.''

The ringing of the telephone caught Leah by surprise. It was only the second time someone had called John's house since she'd been there. The first time it had been her father and stepmother, wanting to let her know they'd arrived safely in London.

Leah had suspected they'd also wanted to know how she was getting along with John, and although they hadn't come right out and asked, she'd kept her conversation light and breezy enough to assure them all was well, even though it hadn't been at the time. They'd promised to call again from Paris, but they weren't due to travel there for another week at least, so it probably wasn't them—

"I'll get it," Gracie sang out.

She grabbed the receiver and voiced a cheery hello, then stood quietly listening to whatever the caller was saying, her expression growing wide-eyed. Leah was about to take the receiver from her in case it was a prank call of some sort when Gracie spoke again in a soft, rather breathless voice.

"She's right here," the little girl said, then pressed the receiver against her chest and whispered to Leah, "It's for you. It's somebody named Kyle. Is he your boyfriend?"

"Kyle?" Leah spoke his name in a whisper of her own.

She wasn't sure whether the flip-flop she'd felt in her belly had resulted from surprised delight or a twist of pain. Six weeks ago she'd thought she'd seen and heard the last of Kyle O'Connor, and also thought it was just as well.

"Do you want to talk to him, Aunt Leah?" Gracie prodded, still whispering.

"Yes, I do," she admitted, as much to herself as to the little girl, for reasons she dared not consider too closely.

She took the receiver from Gracie, her palm damp against the plastic casing, then pressed it to her own chest for several long moments as she tried not only to steady her breathing, but to organize her thoughts. To her relief she realized that any pleasure his telephone call had caused her initially was already being nudged aside by an increasing edge of annoyance she knew she had every right to feel.

"Aren't you going to say anything?" Gracie asked, suddenly concerned.

"Oh, I'm going to say quite a lot, sweetie. Why don't you start on the dishes?"

As Gracie carried her plate to the sink, then stepped up on the stool to rinse it under the faucet, Leah moved to the opposite side of the kitchen, dragging the telephone cord behind her.

"Kyle? Hello. How are you?" she began, trying with some success to keep her tone neutral.

"Leah, darling, how are *you?*"

The dark, smoky sound of his voice took Leah back almost a year, to the day she'd first met him. The headmaster of a school for boys in Chicago, Kyle O'Connor had been attending the same educators' workshop as Leah. They'd ended up sitting side by side at the luncheon and had struck up a conversation easily enough. An attractive, intelligent older man, twenty years her senior, he had flattered her with his interest and attention.

He had sought her out after the workshop ended, as well, and had invited her to have a drink with him. Over glasses of wine in the hotel bar, Leah had found out that he was separated from his wife of eighteen years, that he had two sons, one thirteen, the other sixteen, and that he was as eager as she for the companionship of someone bright and kind and funny.

"I'm fine, Kyle, just fine," Leah replied, firmly setting aside memories of the past.

"I had the devil of a time getting your telephone number. I finally weaseled it out of your landlady. I had to pretend I was desperate, only, I guess I wasn't really pretending.'' He laughed then in a self-deprecating manner, obviously amused at himself, one of his more charming and disarming traits. ''So you've gone back to Montana. Lovely little place to vacation, I suppose. But your landlady said you were planning on staying there all summer. Tell me that's not true, Leah.''

''It's true, Kyle. I'm staying here all summer.'' Leah hesitated, not sure what else she had to say to him, or more accurately, not sure she even *had* anything else to say to him.

She was confused by his sudden interest in her whereabouts and also irritated. He had no right to question how she'd chosen to spend her summer holiday. Nor did he have any right to condemn the choice she'd made.

''I'd much rather have you here, darling.''

''I'm not sure exactly what you're trying to say to me, but the last time we talked, you told me you'd decided to get back together with your wife for the sake of your children,'' Leah reminded him in a matter-of-fact tone. ''I remember the moment quite well. We were having dinner at the Italian restaurant near my apartment building. You were suitably apologetic, but resolute, and I agreed that you were making the right choice.''

Kyle's wife had been the one to file for divorce and the one who had talked of reconciliation almost a year later. Before that, Leah had hoped her relationship with him might eventually end in marriage. She had liked him quite a lot and had thought that love would come as they worked toward building a future together. She had gotten to know his children, and they had seemed to enjoy her company as much as she'd enjoyed theirs.

But once she'd found out that Kyle hadn't rejected out of hand his wife's offer to reconcile, Leah had begun letting go of those hopes and dreams, much as she had done with John when his feelings for Caro had become apparent. Only, she hadn't cared for Kyle nearly as much as she had for John, she acknowledged now. While the end of her relationship with Kyle had saddened her, she had also been somewhat relieved to finally admit that much as she had wished he could be the love of her life, he would never be.

"I realize now that I should have given it more thought," Kyle said. "She's changed and so have I. We talked about it and agreed we might as well stay together for the boys' sake, but she also told me that she doesn't mind if I…see someone else."

Stunned by what he was proposing, Leah couldn't speak for several seconds. Then with an utter sense of calm, she crossed to where the base of the telephone hung on the wall.

"I don't mind, either, Kyle, but that someone isn't going to be me," she said very quietly, then carefully cradled the receiver.

Taking a deep breath, Leah tried to quell the anger building up inside her. Had he really thought she would scurry back to Chicago after a call from him and take on the role of the other woman? Did he honestly believe she valued herself that little?

She hadn't wanted to have only an affair with Kyle O'Connor. She would have never started seeing him in the first place if she hadn't believed that he fully intended to go through with his divorce. Encouraging him to return to his wife hadn't been easy, but she had been convinced that it was best for all concerned at the time. She was even surer of it now.

"Who was that?" Gracie asked from her perch by the kitchen sink.

Wondering how much the little girl had overheard, Leah smiled and shrugged with feigned nonchalance.

"Just a friend of mine calling from Chicago. He wanted to know how I was getting along here in the wilds of Montana, and I told him I was getting along just fine."

"You sounded kind of growly when you were talking to him. Are you mad at him?"

"Disappointed, actually," Leah admitted. "So I sounded growly, huh? As growly as your dad?"

"No, growly like my mom used to sound when she got mad at my dad," Gracie stated simply, her attention seemingly focused on the dish she was rinsing under the faucet.

Leah considered the little girl's comment for several seconds, seeing it as a tentatively offered opening into potentially dangerous territory. Gracie hadn't really said much about her mother in the few days they'd been together. Only that she missed her.

Leah hadn't felt comfortable probing any more deeply into her niece's feelings. Cameron had mentioned that for several months following Caro's death Gracie had gone to a therapist who specialized in treating children who had lost a parent. A few weeks ago the therapist had determined that the little girl had adjusted to the reality of her mother's death as well as could be expected at her age and would no longer need more than an occasional follow-up visit if circumstances warranted.

Now it seemed that her conversation with Kyle, though reasonably low-key, had brought back unhappy memories for her niece.

"Sometimes moms get mad at dads, and dads get mad at moms, too," Leah said, skirting the issue as carefully as she could. "But then they kiss and make up and everybody's happy again. I bet that happens with you and your friends sometimes, too, doesn't it?''

"Tiffany got really mad at me 'cause I cut off all the hair on her Barbie doll, so I let her cut off all the hair on mine, and then she was happy again and so was I. We didn't kiss, but we gave each other a big hug.''

"See? That's what I mean.''

"But my mom didn't want to kiss my dad anymore, Aunt Leah. She just wanted to leave. She said it a lot and then she finally did.''

Startled as much by Gracie's matter-of-fact tone as the revelation she'd made, Leah was momentarily at a loss for words. She and Caro had talked fairly frequently, considering the physical distance separating them, and Caro had come to Chicago to visit quite a few times, first on her own and then with Gracie. Never once had she indicated that she was unhappy in her marriage or that she wanted to leave John, though.

Surely Gracie must be mistaken. But then, Leah remembered what John had said to her Sunday night.

There's a lot you don't know about me. A lot you don't want to know.

She remembered, as well, the tone he'd used. It was as if he hated himself with good reason.

"I bet Kyle wanted you to go back to Chicago, didn't he? Specially since he's your boyfriend, huh?'' Gracie continued. "Then you could kiss and make up.''

"He thought I might consider the idea,'' Leah answered lightly, relieved that her niece had bounced back to their original topic of conversation so easily. "But you know what?''

"What?'' Gracie mimicked with a giggle.

"I told him no way. I'm having too much fun here with my new best friend, and that would be *you*.''

Gracie giggled again, then got down off the stool and opened the door of the dishwasher.

"And you're my new best friend, too, forever and ever."

"And ever," Leah chimed in as she fetched the skillet from the stove, took it to the sink, filled it with soapy water and left it to soak. "Now let's get busy with those flowers that need planting."

The combination of a bright, sunny day with cool breezes blowing and Gracie's cheerful, giggly company helped enormously to soothe Leah's soul. She was done with Kyle O'Connor, no two ways about it, and she had no intention of wasting any more emotional energy on being angry with him. Any mental anguish she experienced while she worked side by side with Gracie in the garden came from thoughts of Caro and John.

Was it possible they hadn't been as blissfully happy together as she'd always assumed? Maybe their marriage had simply hit a bumpy patch as marriages so often do. To a little girl like Gracie, growly-voiced conversations between her parents that lasted more than a day or two could seem scary. And a comment made only once by her mother in an angry moment—a comment about leaving—could sound like an irrevocable decision.

Leah wondered if John was aware of how Gracie remembered the time when Caro was still alive. How frequent had those moments been when Caro was angry with him? What had provoked that emotion in someone who'd always seemed so irrepressible, so effervescent and so joyous? And why hadn't Caro said something to *her* about her feelings when they'd last been together only three months before she died?

All good questions, Leah thought, and all needing to be answered for Gracie's sake, if nothing else. The little girl's dislike of growly voices was certainly understand-able. No child liked to hear the people she loved most talking angrily to each other.

But Gracie seemed to feel that Caro's anger at John, and his at her, had something to do with Caro's death. How that could be possible, Leah didn't know. Caro had died in an automobile accident while driving though a bad storm. A freak accident, her father has said. But no one had ever explained why Caro was out so late with Gracie on such a nasty night.

Until now, Leah hadn't thought to ask. But maybe she should. She didn't want Gracie to continue to believe that Caro's anger at John, her possible desire to leave him and her accidental death were linked if they weren't.

But if they were, then what?

Leah refused to believe in such a possibility. Couples argued. It was just one of many ways they sorted out their problems. A woman, even someone as volatile as Caro could sometimes be, didn't take her child out in the middle of a storm just because she was angry, unless she had a very good reason.

Had something bad been brewing between Caro and John before her death, something that had made an in-delible impression on Gracie? Or had the trauma of los-ing her mother tragically blown a minor disagreement out of proportion in the little girl's mind?

As she gathered up the last of the empty flats that had held the pink-and-white petunias now filling the flower beds on either side of the front door, Leah knew she would have to approach John about the matter. But how to do it and when were important points to consider, she admitted, stuffing the empty flats into the trash bag Gra-cie held open for her.

She would have to approach John very carefully, she

concluded as she remembered again the harsh warning John had given her that first night. And she would best wait a while to do it, too, she added as she caught a glimpse of his Jeep pulling into the driveway a good hour before she'd expected him to be home.

"Look, Aunt Leah, it's my dad!" Gracie said, her pleasure at his early arrival evident in her voice.

"I told you he would be here," she reminded the little girl, experiencing her own thrill of pleasure as she watched John head across the driveway in their direction. There was a slight smile on his handsome face as the breeze lifted his dark, shaggy hair.

"Wait'll he sees how pretty the flower beds look now."

Flashing a grin at Leah, Gracie set out to meet her father. Moving as fast as the brace on her leg would allow, she called, "Daddy, look at all the flowers we planted. Aren't they beautiful? It took us almost the whole day, too. We just finished five minutes ago."

"Talk about perfect timing," he said, scooping his daughter up into his arms. He met Leah's gaze and his smile widened, making her heart beat a little faster. "Looks like you two have been working hard."

"As opposed to someone who's been lounging around a dreary old lab mixing potions and peering into microscopes all day," Leah replied, returning his smile easily despite her wry tone.

"Hey, I might not work up much of a sweat in my lab, but we never lounge around there, either."

"Speaking of working up a sweat..." Leah tugged self-consciously on the damp T-shirt she wore and made a face. "I'd better take a shower before we start dinner. You, too, Gracie, don't you think?"

For just the merest instant, Leah saw a spark of something sexual in John's pale gray eyes. Then he shifted his focus to his daughter.

"I do," he said, wrinkling his nose as he carefully set the little girl on her feet again.

"Am I stinky, Daddy?" she asked with a giggle.

"Very stinky." He waved a hand at the gardening tools and trash bags still scattered around the yard. "You two go inside and get cleaned up. I'll finish putting things away."

"Don't work too hard or you'll end up needing a shower, too," Leah said as she took Gracie by the hand and started past him.

"And that would be a bad thing?" he asked, his teasing voice laced with a velvet undertone.

Startled, Leah glanced back at him and again caught him watching her, a sensually assessing glint in his eyes. As if he was not only imagining her standing under a hot, steamy spray of water, but himself right there with her, she mused.

"Not at all," she managed to reply as she opened the front door and walked inside with Gracie.

Now was definitely not the time to have a potentially confrontational discussion with John, she decided as she sent Gracie upstairs and continued on to her own room. He'd only just begun to accept her presence in his home. More than that, he seemed ready to go a step further and allow himself to enjoy her company. She would be a fool to rock the boat by bringing up the past just yet.

He'd made it clear that he didn't appreciate her meddling in what he considered his personal business. But once he'd gotten used to having her in his life again, once he felt completely comfortable with her, then it might be possible to broach certain subjects, especially if she made it clear she had only Gracie's best interests at heart.

John would want to put his daughter's mind at ease once he knew of her concerns. And he could assure her that no matter how growly their voices had gotten before Caro's death, he and Caro had loved each other—and Gracie—more than anything in the world.

It was the truth, after all. It had to be.

Chapter Six

John made fairly short work of cleaning up the yard, storing the gardening tools and unused bark mulch in the garage and putting the trash bags in the waste can by the back gate. Leah still managed to beat him to the kitchen, though. Obviously she hadn't been inclined to linger in the shower, which was probably just as well. The images in his mind of her standing naked had been vivid enough without the added sound of the shower, which he would have been able to hear, however faintly, anywhere on the first floor of the house.

Much to his relief, she'd also dressed quite modestly, exchanging her short shorts and clinging T-shirt for a plain, loose-fitting, white cotton blouse, sleeves rolled to her elbows, and a pair of equally loose-fitting black cotton pants that came to midcalf. But her feet were bare, and her hair, still damp from the shower, hung to her shoulders in a dark, shiny mass of waves. She hadn't bothered with makeup, but she didn't need any. Her face had a natural sun-kissed glow that made her look younger and lovelier, not to mention sexier, than any artifice ever could.

"Hey," she said as he joined her by the sink.

Her voice was soft and inviting as she glanced at him and smiled tentatively, as if testing his mood for any drastic changes in the fifteen minutes they'd been apart. She was obviously on guard and he had only himself to blame. But that didn't make her hesitancy in his presence any easier to bear. He wished he could erase the bad behavior to which he'd subjected her during the first seventy-two hours she'd been in his home, but he couldn't.

It was probably just as well in the long run, though, John decided. At least now she would think twice, maybe three times, before she poked her nose into his personal business again, and he couldn't help but feel they would both be better off as a result.

"Hey, yourself." He returned her smile, but not too warmly as he washed the grit and grime from his hands. "Anything I can do to help?"

Leah gestured toward the carton of mushrooms on the counter by the sink.

"Rinse those off and slice them."

John set to work as instructed while she removed two large premade pizza shells from their plastic wrappers and arranged each one on a separate cookie sheet.

"You started without me," Gracie complained as she came into the kitchen.

She was dressed in clean blue-and-white-striped shorts and a pale blue T-shirt. Her curls were still dripping from her shower, though, and the look on her face was anything but pleased.

"Oh, Gracie, we're not," Leah assured her. "We were just getting a few things ready for the assembly line." She disappeared into the laundry room, returning a few moments later with a fresh, fluffy, green-and-white-striped towel. "Come here, sweetie, and let me dry off your hair a little bit."

John watched as Leah sat at the table and Gracie climbed into her lap, giggling when Leah scrubbed at her head with the towel. The look on Leah's face was one of undeniable affection. Gracie's place in her aunt's heart was most certainly secure, and vice versa if his daughter's smile was any indication.

He knew that Leah had begun to fill the empty place in his daughter's heart left by Caro's death, but what about Leah? Was Gracie taking the place of the child she wanted but hadn't yet had? Did Leah even want children of her own? Or was she satisfied with the single life she'd led in Chicago the past eight years?

There was so much about Leah that was a mystery to John. After how close they'd once been, he found it hard to believe they'd drifted so far apart.

"Okay, all done," Leah said, taking a moment to finger-comb the little girl's curls into some semblance of order. "Now we can start putting our pizzas together."

With Gracie standing on her stool between them at the counter, they assembled the two pizzas with no small amount of teasing and laughter. First Gracie decorated the pizza shells with sauce from a squeeze bottle. Then she added mushrooms and sliced pepperoni, her favorite toppings, directing Leah and John to hand them to her like a surgeon requesting a scalpel, sutures and scissors.

After generous sprinkles of shredded mozzarella and Parmesan cheese, John maneuvered the pies into the pre-heated oven. Leah poured iced tea into two tall glasses for her and John, and lemonade into another for Gracie, then they waited with increasing impatience for the pizzas to be ready.

"I'm really impressed by how good the yard looks now, front and back," John said, acknowledging his amazement at how the gardens had been transformed by their hard work.

"It helps having the lawn mowed, too," Leah reminded him with a sidelong grin.

"You have to mow every two weeks from now until the first freeze," Gracie added. "That's what Mr. Carey said, didn't he, Aunt Leah?"

"His words exactly."

"Okay, okay, I promise to mow the lawn every two weeks until the first freeze, as per Mr. Carey's instructions. Does that make you happy?" John asked.

"Yes, Daddy," Gracie replied as the timer sounded, reminding them that the pizzas were ready.

Leah didn't answer, busying herself, instead, with finding pot holders and opening the oven door. As she took the first pizza from the oven and set it atop a hot pad on the counter, he picked up the pizza cutter and moved to stand beside her.

"What about you?" he asked softly, pitching his voice for her ears only. "Does that make you happy, too, Leah?"

John didn't want to care one way or another, but he did. Worse still, the more comfortable he became in her presence, the harder it was for him to hide his feelings from her.

She glanced at him in surprise, obviously alerted by something in his tone of voice, then shrugged with studied nonchalance as she bent to retrieve the second pizza.

"A lot happier than I was Sunday night," she said,

then met his gaze again, this time with her smile back in place. "Of course, it wouldn't have taken much for that to happen."

"For what to happen?" Gracie asked, joining them by the counter.

"For me to be happier than I was Sunday night," Leah answered the little girl honestly. "Remember, Gracie, how growly your dad was?"

"Oh, yes, he was so growly Sunday night, but he's been nicer since then, hasn't he?"

"A little nicer," Leah admitted somewhat grudgingly.

"Aunt Leah was growly today, Daddy," Gracie continued, taking a slice of pizza and carrying it on her plate to the table.

From the corner of his eye, John saw Leah go so still she seemed to be holding her breath, and he was instantly curious.

"Aunt Leah, growly? Why was that?" he asked casually, joining his daughter at the table while Leah stayed by the counter, an empty plate gripped in both of her hands.

"Kyle called. He's her boyfriend and she's mad at him," Gracie explained importantly.

Slice of pizza halfway to his mouth, John turned his head to stare at Leah. Gracie's explanation was so far from what he'd expected to hear that he was momentarily rendered speechless. He had assumed at the very worst that one of his nosy neighbors had been a pest again. But Leah's boyfriend calling his house looking for her? And Leah talking to him in a growly voice? His interest had most definitely been piqued.

Apparently galvanized into action, Leah slid a slice of pizza onto her plate and strode to the table.

"I already told you he's not my boyfriend, Gracie," she said, avoiding John's pointed look altogether.

"But you were mad at him, weren't you?" Gracie persisted.

"More disappointed in him than angry, and I told you that, too."

"So who is this guy, anyway?" John asked, his own voice a shade more growly than it had been for several days, and with good reason, he assured himself.

"He's a friend of mine from Chicago," Leah replied, still not looking at him as she cut into her pizza. "He's the headmaster of a school for boys there."

Her cheeks were stained a deep shade of red, which piqued John's curiosity even more. He was about to demand more of an explanation from Leah when Gracie jumped in with a change of subject.

"We're going on a picnic tomorrow, Daddy! Do you want to come with us?"

"Tomorrow?" He frowned thoughtfully, then pushed away from the table and went to check the calendar on the pantry door. "Can't do it tomorrow, sweetie, and neither can you. You have an appointment with Dr. Berry. Her nurse called on Friday while you were at Grandpa's house. She had to change the date of your appointment with Dr. Berry so she could start her vacation a week earlier than originally planned."

"Oh, yes, Dr. Berry." Gracie turned to Leah and giggled. "She's *berry* nice, and after I see her tomorrow, I might not have to wear my brace all the time anymore. Right, Daddy?"

"That's right, Gracie."

"You'll go with us, too, won't you, Aunt Leah?"

"I'd like to, but only if it's all right with your dad."

Leah finally risked a glance in his direction, eyeing him uncertainly.

He wasn't done pursuing the Kyle issue yet. But he would rather attempt to find out more about the man and his relationship with Leah when he had Leah alone. Not that she owed him an explanation. But he damn well wanted one if some guy was calling her at his house and making her angry enough to cause Gracie concern. Not that Gracie had seemed all that concerned. She had actually seemed more fascinated by the fact that her aunt had a boyfriend.

"Of course it's okay," John assured her. "I know you'll want to hear what the doctor has to say about how best to help Gracie get used to walking without the brace."

"That would probably be a good idea," Leah agreed, her blush finally beginning to fade.

Interesting that she was almost as loath as he to discuss personal business, John thought, and he wondered what, if anything, she might have to hide. He would have to make it a point to find out as soon as he could.

"Your appointment is at eleven," he said. "I have to go to the lab first thing tomorrow morning, but I'll pick you up about ten-thirty. If you're especially good, I'll take you out to lunch, but then I'll have to drop you off at home again so I can go back to work for a while."

"I'm always especially good," Gracie said with a proud smile. "At least Dr. Berry always says so." She slipped off her chair and returned to the counter for another slice of pizza, then she added for Leah's benefit, "She likes my dad a lot and he likes her, too."

John suffered a momentary pang of dismay at his daughter's casual remark. But Leah's reaction more than made up for any discomfort he felt. First surprise, then something that looked a lot like disappointment flashed in her green eyes before she quickly lowered her gaze and took another bite of her pizza.

Not that her feelings about him mattered in the long run, but he was oddly relieved to know that she wasn't as unaffected by him in a man-woman kind of way as she'd sometimes seemed the past few days.

"Dr. Berry likes all her patients' parents as long as they're as cooperative as I've been," he explained. "And of course I like her in return because she's taken such good care of Gracie."

"Lucky Dr. Berry," Leah replied brightly as she pushed away from the table. "More tea, John?" Then to Gracie she said, "We can have our picnic for Saturday, instead. How does that sound to you?"

"Perfect," the little girl agreed. "Then Daddy can come with us, too." She looked at him. "'Cause it'll be the weekend and you won't have to work, will you?"

"No, I don't think I will."

John returned to the table and they finished their meal, making plans for the picnic on Saturday. At his suggestion, they decided to drive up to Lolo Pass, a beautiful scenic area reached by a winding road that climbed into the mountains not too far to the west of Missoula.

John hadn't been up there in years. Caro's idea of spending time in the great outdoors had been an afternoon at the country club golf course where she played occasionally during the summer months. He remembered that Lolo Pass had once been a favorite place of Leah's, though. And seeing her eyes light up when he suggested it warmed his heart more than he liked to admit. She was so easy to please, and he really did like pleasing her.

John had hoped to have a more private conversation

with Leah, if not after dinner, then after he'd tucked Gracie into bed. But Leah excused herself after the left-over pizza had been wrapped in foil and stored in the refrigerator and the dishes had been loaded into the dish-washer, making sure first that John would be available to look after Gracie.

He thought she might have plans to go out, which she had every right to do, but instead, she went into her room, closed the door and to his knowledge didn't come out again that night. At least not while he lurked in the kitchen and den, hoping to just happen to be in the right place at the right time, before he finally went to bed.

He would have more than enough time to talk to her about her friend Kyle, John told himself as he went up-stairs just after midnight. If, in fact, the man who had called her was only that. And if he was more than just a friend to Leah…. Then he intended to find out what the man had done to earn her ire. If Kyle had disap-pointed her in some way, then what the hell was she doing even talking to him? Leah shouldn't have to take guff from any man.

Heading down the hallway to his bedroom, John snorted at the ironic twist his thoughts had taken. Leah had been furious with him only a few short days ago because of his mean-spirited behavior toward her. But in her generous and forgiving way, she had given him the benefit of the doubt and stayed around long enough to allow him to come to his senses.

No doubt that was exactly what she would do with her friend, Kyle. And even knowing nothing else about the man except that Leah called him her friend, John admitted he was probably a decent guy and likely more deserving of her understanding than he, himself, would ever be.

Unless Kyle was responsible for another's death—as he was—or had committed some other equally reprehensible act, he would always be the better man for Leah, no matter how much John wished it could be otherwise. He didn't have to like the idea, but he had to accept it for Leah's own good.

He wanted her to be happy, and he wasn't in a position to make that possible for her. Not when all he really had to offer her was disillusionment and heartache.

Leah shifted uncomfortably on the shiny black plastic chair positioned in a corner of the examination room where she, John and Gracie had been taken shortly after their arrival at Dr. Dana Berry's office. Gracie sat bravely on the examination table in the center of the room while John and the doctor stood together, backs to Leah, as the doctor removed the brace from the little girl's leg.

Leah knew it was silly to feel that she'd been purposely excluded from the circle the others had formed. It had seemed to make sense for her to sit in the chair as the doctor directed. The room was small, after all, and if she'd been hovering close by, she would more than likely have been in the way.

Though she didn't take up *that* much space, Leah amended with a wry twist of her lips. And she wouldn't have done anything intentional to deflect John's attention from the doctor. Not that she could have even if she'd tried, she acknowledged.

Dr. Berry was "berry" nice, as Gracie had said. She treated both John and his daughter in a warm and friendly manner. Any dismissal of herself had likely been imagined, Leah decided, aware that on certain occasions under certain circumstances she could be overly sensitive.

And if the doctor's dismissal of her had been intentional, what did it matter? She was Gracie's aunt, visiting for the summer, and as such, she wasn't necessarily someone with whom Dr. Berry would feel the need to cultivate a relationship.

It was the doctor's resemblance to Caro that made Leah feel as if she was standing—well, actually, sitting—in the shadows again. Physically the similarities weren't that noticeable. Although Dr. Berry had blond hair, it was very short and spiked with mousse. She was taller than Caro, too, with a rangy, more athletic build suited to the often physically strenuous manipulation of broken bones that was a necessary part of her chosen medical specialty.

But she had the same confidence, the same carefree effervescence, the same sparkling gaze and easy laugh as Caro. And it was as obvious to Leah as it had been to Gracie that Dr. Dana Berry did, indeed, like John quite a bit, while he, in turn, seemed completely at ease and often outright jocular in her presence.

"I know your left leg looks thin and frail right now, especially compared to your right leg. But the bones are just as strong, maybe ever stronger. They've healed quite well. Now it's time to start getting the muscles back in shape." Dr. Berry turned to John, her already bright smile widening considerably as she instructed, "Lift Gracie down to the floor so she can try taking a few steps without the brace."

"I'm scared," Gracie said, a look of real fear crossing her pale face as she clung to her father.

Leah stood up, thinking only to offer her niece some reassurance, but the doctor waved her away impatiently.

"She's more than ready to walk without the brace. The physical therapist agrees. I suggest fifteen minutes at a time, every two hours today, then thirty minutes tomorrow, adding another thirty minutes every two days, at the most, until she's given up the brace completely," Dr. Berry instructed, then added, "A week from now I doubt she'll want it on at all, and that's fine." She signaled to the little girl with a wave of her hand. "Come on, now, Gracie, let go of your father's hand and take a few steps for me."

Gracie still clung to John, but her gaze met Leah's and locked on pleadingly. Leah knew that the first few steps would be the most difficult for her niece and the most frightening, but that she had to take them sooner or later to complete her recovery. Smiling encouragingly at her, Leah squatted on her heels, held out her arms and nodded once in reassurance.

Taking a quick breath, Gracie let go of her father's hand and slowly, gingerly, closed the distance between her and Leah, her eyes locked on Leah's all the way. When she finally stopped in front of her, Leah put her arms around the little girl and hugged her close.

"Good job, Gracie," she murmured, blinking back the tears that stung her eyes. "I'm so proud of you."

"Thanks, Aunt Leah."

"Now walk back to your father so I can put your brace on again," Dr. Berry said.

"I don't want it on right now," Gracie replied with a smile and a brave tip of her chin. "I want to walk out to the car without it today."

"Okay, Gracie, but don't overdue it the next few days, or your leg will end up sore and possibly swollen." Dr. Berry flicked a glance at Leah. "You will make sure she takes it easy, won't you, Ms. Hayes? You are looking after her for the summer, right?''

"Yes to both questions," Leah answered as she put her arm around her niece's shoulders and stood up.

"That must leave you with some added free time," the doctor said to John, favoring him with another of her brilliant, not to mention unabashedly inviting, smiles.

"Not a lot," he replied, returning her smile with warmth, but no real indication of interest that Leah could see. "They've had me working out in the yard at home, and they have a picnic planned for tomorrow."

"Sounds like fun," Dr. Berry acknowledged, managing to sound so wistful that Leah was afraid she might invite herself along before she added, "I'll be on my way to New York then."

"Right, you're taking some vacation time, aren't you," John said.

"A month," she confirmed. "I'd really like to see you when I get back, though."

"I'll make an appointment for Gracie on the way out," John replied, either unaware of or ignoring what the doctor seemed—at least to Leah—to be implying.

"That will be fine. See you in four weeks, then," she said, looking just the tiniest bit annoyed.

"See you," Gracie piped up as John tucked her brace under his arm and opened the door of the examination room so they could exit.

"Nice meeting you, Dr. Berry," Leah said, trying not to gloat. "Enjoy your vacation."

"Nice meeting you, too, Ms. Hayes, and you enjoy your summer here."

"I'm sure I will."

"Where is it you'll be returning to in August?"

"Chicago," Leah replied.

"Nice city."

"Yes, very nice."

As she and Gracie waited for John to make the appointment, Leah wondered if Dr. Berry planned to start her pursuit of him before or after she left Missoula. Then she wondered why she cared, since she wouldn't be here once the summer was over, anyway. No doubt Dr. Berry's attention would be good for John. She was certainly his type, and she seemed to like Gracie well enough. Though Leah doubted her profession would leave her much time to spend with another man's child, she wouldn't be intentionally unkind to her.

For just a moment Leah thought maybe she should suggest as much to him, but only for a moment. If John was interested in the doctor, he was more than capable of going after her on his own. He didn't need any help from her. And if he was interested...

Much as she wanted John to find happiness and knowing as she did that it could never be with her, Leah admitted that she would just as soon not have to watch their mating dance. In fact, watching John court Dana Berry was right at the top of the list of things she'd rather never have to do—tied for first place with answering his questions about Kyle.

He had dropped the subject at dinner last night, hopefully for good. She hadn't really been able to gauge his interest, so she couldn't be sure. But with luck, it had only been fleeting and already forgotten.

"Can we go someplace for lunch?" Gracie asked as they slowly made their way to John's Jeep, accommodating the little girl's tentative steps. "I was especially good, wasn't I?"

"*Especially* good," John assured her, an odd note in

his voice catching Leah's attention. "Where would you like to go?"

"The Diner, please," she replied without hesitation, naming a popular restaurant in downtown Missoula.

"The Diner it is, then."

Glancing at John, Leah saw that his gaze was focused on his daughter. There was a grim twist to his lips as he watched Gracie's determined progress across the small parking lot. Although it had been almost a year since the accident, Leah had a feeling it was on John's mind now, stark and vivid as he faced yet again all that he and Gracie had lost. And he blamed himself, Leah acknowledged.

But he couldn't have any reason to, could he? Unless something *had* happened between him and Caro that fateful night, as Gracie had seemed to suggest.

"Have you ever been to the Diner, Aunt Leah?" the little girl asked as they waited for John to open the car doors for them.

"Many times," she replied. "They have the best chocolate shakes in town, don't they, John?"

"Yeah, sure." His voice flat, he lifted his daughter onto the back seat and buckled her seat belt.

"I like their grilled cheese sandwiches a lot," Gracie said, seemingly unaware of her father's shift in mood.

"And I like their chili pie." Leah grinned at the little girl, at the same time reaching out and giving John's arm a gentle squeeze.

He glanced at her questioningly and seemed ready to snarl at her, but the pleading look she sent him must have registered, for he kept silent. He appeared to give himself a mental shake, then gently freed himself from her grasp to cross to the driver's-side door.

"The meat loaf and mashed potatoes sound good to

me today," he said, his voice cheerful enough again to ease her concerns at least a little.

The Diner was bustling with the usual lunchtime crowd, bolstered by summer tourists stopping on their way to Flathead Lake and Glacier National Park north of town. Luckily a family was leaving just as John, Leah and Gracie arrived, and they were able to claim a booth by one of the windows overlooking the street without having to wait. They seated themselves, but didn't bother with menus, each of them ordering their favorite meal and each of them splurging on a chocolate shake.

John paid special attention to Gracie while they waited for their food to arrive, making sure that her leg hadn't started to ache in a way that made her uncomfortable. The little girl had asked if she could give up the brace until they were home again, and since they would be sitting down to eat, both Leah and John had acquiesced to her wishes.

Once realizing that her leg was strong enough to bear her weight without buckling, Gracie's confidence had grown enormously. Leah wondered if she would be wearing the brace at all in two days' time, rather than the week Dr. Berry had predicted.

The chili pie was as good as Leah remembered and she ate every bite. Gracie, too, finished her grilled cheese sandwich and fries with obvious relish. But John ate only a small portion of his meat loaf and mashed potatoes.

"It was very good, really," he told the waitress when she expressed her concern and handed him a take-out carton. "I'm just not as hungry as I thought I was."

Recalling that he had eaten only a bowl of cereal at seven that morning and knowing his appetite was usually more hearty, Leah eyed him questioningly. He studiously avoided her gaze, however, as he transferred the bulk of his meal from plate to plastic carton.

Despite his efforts to make their time together pleasant, John still seemed to have something upsetting on his mind. And there was no way she could ease his worries when she didn't have a clue as to what it involved.

"Can I ask Tiffany to come over and play when we get home?" Gracie asked as they headed back to the house.

"Sounds fine to me," Leah said. "Is it okay with you, John?"

"Yes, it's fine with me, too. Of course, I won't be there to lend a hand with them if they get too silly. I have to go back to the lab."

"I'm reasonably sure I'll be able to manage on my own," Leah said.

"We'll be really good, Daddy, I promise," Gracie added.

"I know you will." He glanced back at her and gave her a loving smile as he pulled to a stop in the driveway.

"Will we see you later?" Leah asked. Trying not to sound too hopeful, she picked up Gracie's brace and opened the car door.

"Probably late tonight. Otherwise, I won't be able to take time off for our picnic tomorrow," he replied without meeting her gaze. "So don't wait dinner for me."

Leah suspected that John was using work as an excuse to distance himself from her and Gracie again, but with Gracie sitting right there with them, she didn't dare say as much to him. In fact, she had been just as guilty of using her own variation of avoidance during their conversation last night. Accusing him of behaving in a like manner wouldn't do her, or more important, Gracie, any good. He would go to the lab and stay there well into the evening regardless of what she said or did.

"What time would you like to leave for Lolo Pass tomorrow morning?" she asked.

"How about eight-thirty? That's not too early, but we'll still miss some of the tourist traffic."

"We'll be ready then," Leah agreed as she helped Gracie out of the Jeep.

"Bye, Daddy," the little girl called out.

"Bye, sweetie." He met Leah's gaze finally, if only for the briefest moment. "Thanks, Leah," he added as he put the Jeep into reverse. "I appreciate...everything you're doing for us."

"Hey, that's what friends are for," she reminded him cheerfully. "Don't work too hard."

She closed the car door, then turned to follow Gracie up the sidewalk to the front door as John backed out of the driveway.

"I think I need to put my brace on again," Gracie said after they'd gone into the house.

"Leg feeling a little achy, huh?"

"Just a little. But I still feel good enough to play with Tiffany."

"I never doubted that for a moment," Leah teased the little girl. "Let's call her mom and see if she can come over."

Tiffany's mother was more than happy to allow her daughter to play at Gracie's house. Together, the little girls later decided a sleepover might be fun, especially if Tiffany could also join them on their picnic the following day.

Leah agreed, knowing how much Gracie needed the company of her best friend as she continued to celebrate giving up her brace. So did Tiffany's mother, who gladly brought over a small backpack filled with clothes and various other items she thought Tiffany might need for their excursion.

To ensure the girls actually got some sleep, Leah had them camp out in their sleeping bags on the floor of her room. When John hadn't come home by ten, she left a note for him explaining the slight change of plans and sleeping arrangements so he wouldn't panic when he saw that Gracie wasn't in her room as usual.

She was dozing sometime around midnight, not quite able to sleep soundly with John still out, when she heard him come into the kitchen at last. With a sigh of relief, she snuggled into her pillow and closed her eyes. She was almost asleep when she heard the door of her room open ever so quietly.

Eyes open once more, Leah caught a glimpse of John standing hesitantly in the doorway. Thinking he might need her for some reason, she was about to let him know that she was awake, but almost immediately he backed out of her room again, shutting the door as quietly as he'd opened it.

He had simply acted in a normal, fatherly manner, checking on Gracie, Leah told herself. Still, she couldn't help but feel that she had been included in his concern, as well. Even in the darkness, she had seen his gaze move from the two girls sleeping on the floor to the bed where she lay and then linger there.

A small thing, really, but it meant a lot to Leah to know he really did care about her, despite the distance he insisted on maintaining most of the time they were together. And small things could grow and change if one made an effort to nurture them.

She and John had been apart a long time, and their lives had changed a lot in the intervening years. In addition, the circumstances bringing them together again had been anything but the best. But their newly forged relationship had already begun to show signs of improvement. They were actually talking to each other without snarling, and with Gracie as a buffer, they had shared several activities.

Maybe sometime soon John would stop withdrawing altogether, and they could once again enjoy the comfort of the friendship they had shared in the past. She'd be going back to Chicago at the end of the summer to resume her life, and he would be staying in Missoula with his daughter. But knowing she'd regained his affection, she'd always be able to return for a visit, and she would be happy enough with that prospect. She would have to be.

Chapter Seven

The one thing John hadn't considered when he saw Leah's note saying that Gracie's friend would be joining them on their outing to Lolo Pass was that he'd be able to have some time alone with Leah. Well, not exactly alone, since the two girls were always reasonably close by and there were other families enjoying the area, as well. But sitting with her on an old quilt in a patch of sun-dappled shade under a stand of trees, while Gracie and Tiffany giggled together as they played with their dolls on another quilt several yards away, he had her all to himself, more or less.

Part of him wished it was more, and another part of him, equally strong, wished it was less—the same old conflict rearing its same old ugly head. To be with Leah in all ways possible or not to be...

The day had started out better than he'd expected. The moodiness that had descended on him the previous af-

ternoon as they'd left Dr. Berry's office had lifted somewhat, though it had yet to vanish altogether. Seeing Gracie trying so hard to be brave as she took her first
tentative steps without the brace she'd worn for the past
several months had again reminded him of the hand he'd
played in her current condition.

In flashes, one after another, he remembered the night
of the accident, Caro rushing to her car with Gracie, half-
asleep, clutched in her arms. Then seeing Caro again as
the doctor drew back the sheet covering her surprisingly
serene face. And finally coming upon his daughter in
another cubicle of the emergency room mere moments
before she was to be wheeled away to the operating
room. Her face had been terrifyingly pale and her left
leg a torn, bloody mess.

She'd spent weeks in the hospital recuperating. Her
slow recovery at home had followed, punctuated by trips
to the physical therapist to help her start walking again,
and other trips to the psychologist to help her deal with
the loss of her mother. All because of his stubborn insistence that he wouldn't, under any circumstance, allow
Caro to end their marriage.

John had worked doggedly in the lab yesterday afternoon and evening, immersing himself in the scientific
study he loved until those painful memories of the past
finally began to recede. Exhausted by the time he eventually headed home again, he was able to sleep the night
through and awake ready to make the day a good one
for his daughter, Tiffany and, of course, Leah.

At his suggestion, they'd stopped for coffee and juice,
bagels and doughnuts on their way out of town, the
lunch Leah had packed stowed in the rear cargo area of
the Jeep. He had driven along the winding road at a
moderate speed, stopping several times so they could

walk along the sparkling river, still running high with the snowmelt coming off the mountains. It was a cool, clear day, the kind of day when Montana truly earned its sobriquet of Big Sky Country.

They'd reached Lolo Pass early enough to find a parking place convenient to the picnic area. Still full from breakfast, though, they'd opted to explore the visitors' center, then take a short hike along one of the many trails leading to various scenic overlooks before digging into their lunch.

At John's insistence, Gracie had reluctantly worn her brace for the hike and had managed quite well over the rough, rocky terrain. Once back at the picnic area, however, she had taken it off and left it off, getting around without any obvious problems.

They had all eaten Leah's chicken sandwiches, tossed salad, sliced fruit and chocolate-chip brownies with great gusto. Then the little girls had set up their own "camp," leaving John and Leah to enjoy a last glass of wine from the bottle she'd so thoughtfully tucked into the cooler, along with a jug of lemonade.

Neither of them had said much during the few minutes they'd been alone together. John wondered if Leah was searching as frantically as he was for a relatively safe topic of conversation. Or maybe she was just as content as he was to sit back, relax and enjoy the peaceful time they were finally able to share with each other.

"They are so cute together, aren't they?" Leah asked, finally breaking the silence.

She sat with her back against a tree trunk, her jean-clad legs stretched out in front of her.

"They've been best friends since they were three years old. They went to the same preschool program and gravitated toward each other on the very first day. They

like a lot of the same things, but they have enough differences of opinion to keep it interesting,'' he replied as
he braced a palm on the quilt and leaned back to better
enjoy the small patches of sunshine drifting through the
tree branches.

"Gracie told me about the day she cut Tiffany's doll's
hair. Tiffany was so mad at her that Gracie let Tiffany
cut her doll's hair, too. Then they were friends again.''

"I laughed when I first heard about the Barbie inci-
dent, as it came to be known,'' John said. "But I was
also pretty amazed at how they found a way to get past
it that seemed fair to both of them.'' Smiling, he looked
over at Leah. "I'm surprised she mentioned it, though.
It's been a while since it happened—almost two years,
in fact.''

"We were talking about how two people can be angry
at each other for a while, but then they care enough
about their friendship or their marriage or whatever, to
find a way to let the anger go,'' Leah replied, holding
his gaze.

"Sounds to me like a pretty deep discussion to have
with a six-year-old.''

Feeling a sudden sense of trepidation, John shifted so
that he was sitting cross-legged. He focused on the wine
still remaining in his glass, swirling it slightly so it glim-
mered in the sunlight. He wanted to ask what had
brought on such a serious conversation between Leah
and his daughter, but he wasn't sure he wanted to know
the answer. In any case, he had a feeling Leah wouldn't
let the subject drop if she had more to say, and she
immediately proved him right.

"Actually, Gracie was the one who brought up the
subject. She said some things about you and Caro—

things that concerned me," Leah explained in a quiet, nonaccusatory tone.

"What things?" he asked, his own concern for Gracie outweighing his determination not to discuss with Leah any aspects of his relationship with Caro.

"She said that you and Caro used growly voices a lot of the time when you talked to each other."

John heard the hesitancy in Leah's voice. She didn't like poking into his private business any more than he liked having her do it. But obviously she thought it was necessary for Gracie's sake. Well, he would offer her a few standard platitudes and hope she'd be satisfied.

"All married people have arguments, Leah, as I'm sure you know. Disagreeing, even in growly voices, doesn't mean anything, really. Although I can understand how it might have upset Gracie if she overheard us occasionally, as she seems to have done. She's always been an especially tenderhearted little girl."

"She said her mother talked about leaving you," Leah continued, seeming to ignore his carefully worded explanation. "And she seems to think her mom's intention to leave you had something very important to do with the car accident."

John's gut twisted painfully as he realized for the first time how much his daughter must have overheard and understood, not to mention remembered about what had happened the night Caro died. He'd assumed the little girl had been asleep during the worst of his final argument with Caro. He'd also assumed that when Caro left the house with her, Gracie, pulled from her bed as she was, had still been mostly asleep.

But he wasn't about to reveal those assumptions to Leah. He would only be opening the door to questions he had no intention of ever answering. Better to act as if he didn't know what Leah was talking about, to chalk up Gracie's concerns as another result of the stormy night and the general confusion it created where the accident was concerned.

He would talk to Gracie privately and offer her the reassurance she not only seemed to need, but also deserved to have from him. But he would do it on his own. There was no need to involve Leah.

"She's never mentioned any concerns like that to me," he said, which was true enough. "Now that I know what she's been thinking, though, I'll do what I can to put her mind at ease."

John swallowed the last of his wine in a quick gulp, then risked a glance at Leah. A frown furrowed her lovely brow and he could almost hear the little wheels turning in her head. She didn't seem willing to drop the subject, so he took it upon himself to initiate an abrupt change of tack, instead. There were a few things he'd been meaning to find out about her himself.

"Gracie's interest in anger management, or lack thereof, wouldn't have been precipitated by that call you got from your friend, Kyle, would it?" he asked, putting into words the first thought that had come to mind.

The slight blush that tinted Leah's cheeks was all the response he really needed, but she also answered him in the affirmative.

"I suppose it was," she admitted, though with noticeable reluctance. "I should have been more careful about the tone I used, especially since I wasn't really all that angry, but rather, as I keep saying, disappointed. I explained all that to Gracie at the time, though."

"Disappointed, huh?" John shifted on the quilt again, this time so that he faced Leah fully. "Why was that?"

She shrugged and looked past him to where Gracie and Tiffany still played together contentedly.

"It's not important. He won't be calling me again."

"He won't?"

John was intrigued by the way Leah hedged in her replies. It seemed likely to him that Kyle had been more than just a friend of hers at one time. Otherwise, she would surely have been more forthright about her relationship with him.

"No, he won't." She, too, drained the last of her wine, then twisted the glass from side to side in her hand.

"So why did he call you in the first place?"

He really should drop the subject, John thought, noting the way Leah's lips tightened into a thin line. But he couldn't seem to do it. And his interest had little to do with Gracie's well-being. It had become strictly personal now.

"He had something he wanted to tell me," Leah replied, suddenly sounding just the slightest bit snappish. "Something personal, okay? Not that it's any of your business one way or another."

"Hey, I'm only interested in what you've been up to the past eight years," he said, acknowledging the wisdom of changing tack yet again. "Caro kept me up-to-date on some of what was happening in your life, but she was never one to waste a lot of time on details. Your friend Kyle was obviously a new development. I hadn't heard his name mentioned until the other day. I was just curious."

"He's a touchy subject for me right now," Leah admitted, sounding somewhat mollified. She met John's gaze at last, smiled slightly and shrugged again. "Okay?"

"Okay." John smiled, too. "So how has living in Chicago been for you otherwise?"

"I like it," she replied, although with less enthusiasm than he would have expected, considering how long she'd lived there. "I enjoy teaching at St. Augusta's— most of the time, at least. The girls are pretty well-behaved by today's standards. Most of the time, it's the parents who cause the problems."

"You like living in a big city?"

"I've gotten used to it."

Again Leah's response lacked the fervor he'd expected.

"I guess what I'm really trying to find out is whether you miss living in Missoula. You always seemed so content here as a kid. I never thought you'd end up making a life for yourself in a big city so far from home."

"I do miss being here, actually," she admitted. "I miss the slower pace of life, and I miss…" She waved a hand to include the pristine beauty of the picnic area and the mountain glade surrounding it. "I miss being able to hop in the car and drive to a place as remote and lovely as this for the day. I miss the easy access to skiing in the winter and hiking in the mountains in the summer. I miss—" her voice trailed off as she gazed into the distance "—a lot of things."

"You could always move back to Missoula," he said, surprised at how much he wanted her to agree. "The schools here are always in need of good science teachers. And you still have friends here, as well as your father…and Gracie and me."

"My life is in Chicago now," she replied with only the merest hint of hesitation. "I have a good job, a nice apartment, people I care about. I would have to start all over again in Missoula."

"Would that be so difficult?"

Again John surprised himself with the insistence he heard in his voice. He couldn't understand it, either. What did he expect to happen if Leah moved back to Missoula?

Having her in the same town on a permanent basis without really being able to have her in his life in the intimate way he wanted would likely drive him crazy. And having to watch firsthand as some other man dated her and eventually won her love would be more than he could bear.

Better by far to let her go back to Chicago where he wouldn't have to witness on a daily basis just how easily she could live happily ever after without him.

"Probably not, but I'm happy there, happy enough to stay, at least for now."

"Do you have anyone special in your life, aside from the not-to-be-mentioned Kyle, of course?" He wasn't sure he wanted to know the answer. Still he couldn't help but ask, considering the path his thoughts had taken. "Caro never mentioned anything much about your love life. I'm assuming you've had one."

Leah shot him a look that reflected in equal measure both her exasperation at his merciless probing and her good-natured resignation.

"Don't be shy, John," she chided him with a wry smile. "Just ask me the most personal questions possible, sit back, grinning, and expect me to give you answers."

"Well, Leah, you told me all about your crush on Stewart Danner," he reminded her, recalling that he'd been jealous of her affection for the eighth grader, but had never let her know it.

"That was years ago. I was in seventh grade, terribly

shy and gawky, and Stewart was a year ahead of me. I remember hoping you'd put in a good word for me, one older man to another, so to speak. But I don't think you did, did you.''

"You might have been shy, but you were never gawky. As for Stewart, he was a jerk," John replied, avoiding a direct response to her question. "You deserved better."

"I know that now, but back then, I thought he hung the moon."

Once again Leah stared off into the distance, her smile taking on a wistful cast.

"And what was I? Chopped liver?" John demanded of her only half-teasingly.

"You were my good buddy, years older and not the least bit inclined to think of me as main-squeeze material," she replied, reminding him how successful he'd been at hiding his real feelings from her, especially in those months before Caro had come into their lives.

He had been so afraid of scaring her away by coming on too strong. Though mature for her age in some ways due to her mother's death, she had been naive about so many other things. Unbeknownst to her, he had been waiting for just the right time to begin her initiation into the physical aspects of love.

Then he'd met Caro, who was so worldly-wise, so sophisticated and so sure of what she wanted that he'd been dazzled. Too dazzled by her to realize what he was giving up in the bargain.

"So you're saying there hasn't been anyone you've desired since Stewart Danner? Who, by the way, lives in Seattle and designs computer software for a living."

"You've kept up with Stewart?" Leah quirked an eyebrow at him.

"He's one of the university's most celebrated alumni. His latest achievements are front-page features in our newsletter. But enough about Stewart—"

"Okay, okay," Leah conceded. She set her wineglass aside, took a deep breath and looked away, a thoughtful expression on her face. "I met a guy my freshman year at Northwestern. Austin Bradley III, or IV…I could never remember, which should have told me something right there. But I digress."

She shot John a smile, then continued with her recitation.

"We started out as good friends. He was in my organic-chemistry class and he was having a terrible time, so I offered to be his study partner. He had a girlfriend, someone he'd grown up with in Dallas. Her family was just as prominent as his family, but she had chosen to attend Brown, instead of Northwestern.

"Anyway, long story short, the girlfriend met another guy, broke up with Austin, and Austin and I started dating. We got pretty serious for a while. I met his family and Bethany—the former girlfriend—and *her* family, and they were all very nice to me. But I never felt that Austin really loved me. He liked me well enough, but he didn't…cherish me.

"Midway through our senior year, during our Christmas holiday, he and Bethany got together again in Dallas. It was really the best thing that could have happened for all of us. They were certainly better suited to each other, and last I heard they were expecting their first child."

Though Leah's tone remained matter-of-fact throughout the telling of her story, John noted the wistful look in her eyes. As pragmatic as she seemed determined to be about her relationship with Austin Bradley, he sensed that she'd hoped at one time that it would have a different ending—one that possibly would have involved a happily-ever-after for her and Austin together.

But Austin had chosen Bethany to be his wife, and Leah had moved graciously off to the sidelines. Much as she had done when her father met Georgette and no longer needed her in quite the same way. And, John realized with sudden insight, much as she had done when he had fallen head over heels for Caro eight years ago.

Had Leah gotten caught in a pattern of some sort where men were concerned? Had she somehow programmed herself to step aside rather than to fight for what she wanted?

But that seemed highly unlikely for several reasons, John thought. It had only been natural for a daughter like Leah to be glad that her father had found a woman with whom to share a life of peace and happiness, thus freeing her to make a life of her own. And he and Leah had only been friends before Caro had come into their lives—very good friends, true, but never more than that. And they had remained close friends during his courtship of Caro.

As far as he knew, Leah had never thought of him in a romantic way and was genuinely happy for him and Caro when they'd announced their engagement. She'd done no real stepping aside there, at least none to his knowledge. In fact, the only way that could have happened was if she'd hidden certain feelings from him— feelings he'd been previously unaware of—when he'd allowed his own feelings for Caro to become so obvious.

"And after Austin…Kyle?" John asked, even more interested in her relationship with the man who'd called the house and disappointed her enough that she'd used a growly voice with him.

"The not-to-be-mentioned Kyle," she reminded him quietly as she began to gather up the remains of their picnic lunch.

"So what happened with him? Did he have an old girlfriend, too?" John asked teasingly.

The pained look in her eyes as she met his gaze for one long moment made him wish he'd dropped the subject altogether. But at the same time he was more curious than ever about the obvious hold the man had over her emotions. Selfishly he was glad Austin Bradley had had a girlfriend to go back to in Dallas, and he hoped Kyle O'Connor was out of Leah's life for good, as well. But only Leah could tell him that for sure.

"Kyle was, actually *is,* a friend of mine, nothing more, nothing less," she stated, evading a direct answer to his question. Then, shifting her attention, Leah called out to the two girls still playing quietly together, "Gracie, Tiffany, start gathering your things. Otherwise we won't have enough time to hike along another of the trails for a little while before we have to head back home."

Aware that he would have to save any further interrogation about Leah's personal relationships until another time, John helped her pack the remains of their lunch in the cooler. He also helped her fold the quilts while the little girls sorted out their dolls and related paraphernalia.

They again chose one of the less-strenuous trails for their afternoon hike, and after Gracie strapped on her brace, they headed off in a different direction than they had earlier. There were quite a few other people hiking the same trail, increasing the traffic considerably, and the girls stayed close by, affording John no private moments with Leah.

But just being with her in the quiet, woodsy setting, having her walking close beside him at a rhythmic pace that matched his own, her boots scrunching the dry leaves and pine needles covering the path, filled him with an unaccountable sense of peace and contentment.

Without really pausing to consider the effect of such an action, he reached out, took Leah's hand in his and gave it a gentle squeeze meant to reassure her. She glanced up at him, a startled look on her face, then held his gaze, an unspoken question in her eyes.

"Having fun?" he asked, relieved when she hadn't immediately pulled her hand from his grasp.

"Lots of fun," she replied. "And you?"

"Lots of fun, too."

He gave her hand another gentle squeeze, savoring the tactile contact, however slight. He would have liked even better to put his arm around her shoulders. And even better than that, to back her up against a tree and claim her lovely, luscious mouth in a deeply demanding kiss.

"I can't believe you and Caro never came up here with Gracie. It's the perfect place for hiking in the summer and cross-country skiing in the winter," Leah said.

"Actually, the snowmobiles take over in the winter now," he replied. "As for coming up here with Caro…she wasn't one for hiking or skiing. She wasn't much interested in my work, either, and small-town life in general seemed to bore her, too."

Once started on the list of disappointing differences he'd discovered between him and Caro as their marriage progressed, John couldn't seem to stop himself. He had kept to himself his dissatisfaction with their very basic and unchangeable incompatibility for what he now considered too many years. In fact, he'd been so unwilling to be disloyal to her even in his thoughts that he hadn't faced the reality of their situation until she'd begun to throw her own unhappiness in his face with increasing regularity.

"It's not that unusual for couples to enjoy different activities," Leah pointed out, giving *his* hand a reassuring squeeze. "I've even heard that it can really be quite healthy."

John wanted to tell her that in the weeks leading up to Caro's death, there hadn't been anything healthy at all about his marriage, but he managed to keep that particular thought to himself. Leah already had enough questions about their relationship. No need to add more fuel to that fire, and keeping Caro in the conversation would definitely do just that.

"Did you and Kyle enjoy different activities, too?" he asked, shifting back to the one subject guaranteed to deflect any further probing she might have in mind herself just then.

He normally hated playing tit for tat, but under the circumstances it promised to provide a much-needed smoke screen.

"Sometimes," she admitted, scowling at him, then pulled her hand from his grasp, ostensibly to look at her watch, but, John suspected, more to signal her displeasure with him. "It's almost four o'clock. I think we'd better start heading back."

John called out to Gracie and Tiffany, and with the girls again just ahead of them, they retraced their steps to the parking lot. He considered taking Leah by the hand once more, then thought better of it. Even that small intimacy seemed unwise at the moment.

It was becoming much too easy for him to let down his guard with her when they were together. It was also obvious that any additional bond drawing them closer could very well have him on the verge of telling all.

He didn't want to consider what Leah would think of him once she knew the truth about him and Caro, but of course he had. And he clung to that consideration now, determined to avoid saying anything that would disappoint her or, even more likely, disgust her.

They made the return trip to Missoula in noticeably shorter time than their outward-bound journey had taken. At John's suggestion, they stopped at a little roadside café for an early dinner, thus sparing Leah and him the necessity of fixing something when they finally got home. After some minor fussing from the two increasingly tired little girls, they dropped Tiffany off at her house, a stop that ended up also entailing having a glass of wine with her parents so they could renew their acquaintance with John and get to know Leah.

Home at last, Leah shooed John and Gracie upstairs so she could unpack the cooler while he helped his daughter get ready for bed. By the time he'd tucked a very grumpy Gracie into bed, read her the story she chose and returned to the kitchen, it was empty. Moving into the den, he could see that the door to Leah's room was closed, as good an indication as any that she'd decided to call it a night.

Knowing he would be wise to do the same, John went back up to his study. He thought about reading one of the many professional journals stacked on his desk collecting dust, but he was too tense and too restless to sit still for more than a few minutes at a time. Instead, he prowled around the house, making no effort to be quiet in the hope that Leah would hear him and come out of her room to investigate.

Though where he expected that to lead he didn't dare consider too closely.

Only, he couldn't help thinking about running into her in the dimly lit kitchen—Leah in that short, black T-shirt she slept in, and him in sweatpants, his chest bare...

With a groan of disgust, John ran upstairs again, pulled on a sweatshirt, a pair of socks and running shoes, and grabbed his keys. Outside in the clear, cold dark of a Montana summer night, the stars twinkling overhead and the moon glowing fat and full, he set off at a steady pace down the deserted sidewalk.

He would stay out of the house until he'd walked off whatever was ailing him, not to mention addling his brain. And only when he was too exhausted to do anything but sleep would he return home again. No matter how desperately he wanted Leah in every intimate way imaginable, he had to stay away from her. He owed her that consideration and so much more, for old time's sake if nothing else.

Chapter Eight

Sunday morning Leah sat alone at the kitchen table trying to give the various newspapers to which John subscribed the attention they deserved. She'd set aside the *New York Times,* too daunted by its sheer size to tackle it just yet. Instead, she'd started with the *Missoulian,* scanning it slowly for local news and finding several articles of interest, including one on the proposed closing of a major road in Glacier National Park to facilitate repairs.

The *Seattle Post* also offered up some intriguing ideas for things to do during a long weekend in the city, a getaway Leah thought Gracie might enjoy. Seattle was a fairly easy and interesting eight-hour drive away. She and Gracie could go on their own, or she could mention the trip to John as something the three of them might do together.

If he ever put in an appearance, she thought, looking

at the clock on the microwave oven and seeing it was almost eight-thirty. Gracie, too, for that matter, though Leah could understand why they were sleeping late after the physically tiring day they'd had. She wished she'd been able to stay in bed longer that morning herself, especially since she'd had an impossible time falling asleep the night before.

Leah had gone to her room while John was still upstairs with Gracie, determined to avoid any more of his probing questions about her personal relationships. She'd been honest enough with him about Austin Bradley. Austin had been someone she'd cared for, but he was not the love of her life. She could admit that now, along with her belief that he and Bethany had always belonged together, even though she'd been hurt by his abandonment during their senior year at Northwestern. She hadn't minded telling John about him in the least, though.

Kyle was another matter, however. She'd made a big mistake getting involved with him before his divorce was final. An even bigger mistake than she'd realized when he called her the other day. And she didn't want to share the embarrassing details with John—details he seemed much too interested in ferreting out.

Though safe enough from John behind the closed door of her room, Leah still hadn't been able to settle down. The space that should have been her sanctuary had seemed more like a cage. She'd found herself either pacing from end to end or staring out the window into the darkness, longing for who knew what more times than she cared to count. And it wasn't so much what John wanted to know about Kyle that had her mind spinning, but what John had intimated about his relationship with Caro.

Obviously they'd gone their separate ways more than Caro had ever indicated to her during their supposedly heart-to-heart discussions the times the two of them had been together. Or maybe, Leah thought, she just hadn't picked up on some of the comments her stepsister had made or some of the signals she'd likely given when she'd come to visit her in Chicago.

Caro had loved being in the city. She'd talked constantly about how exciting it was in Chicago compared to Missoula, and, impossible as it had seemed to Leah, she hadn't been all that enthusiastic about going home again, especially the last few times she'd come to visit. But to Leah, going home to John would have been more exciting and more rewarding than anything Chicago would ever have had to offer.

Nothing Leah could imagine, in fact, would have been better than having John's love and devotion. And she'd truly believed that despite her occasional murmurs of discontent, Caro had returned that love and devotion in complete and equal measure.

There'd been a bitter undertone in John's voice when he'd listed the ways in which he and Caro had differed, though. Had familiarity bred contempt between the two of them under the surface of what Leah had always considered their perfect marriage? Had Caro really been that desperately unhappy with John? And more important had John also been desperately unhappy with Caro?

Then why stay together?

For Gracie's sake of course, Leah had answered herself. John had suffered greatly during his parents' bitter, angry, hurtful divorce. He would never have put his own daughter through a similar experience if he could help it. Not that a divorce had to be as awful as the one between his parents had been.

But what if Caro had wanted to take Gracie to another city in another, likely distant, state? John would never have allowed that to happen, because he wouldn't have been able to bear being parted from her for the long stretches of time that would have resulted.

Her mind whirling with one question on top of another, Leah had tossed and turned in her bed most of the night. By the time sleep finally claimed her, she'd come to the conclusion that any answers she found were now beside the point. Caro had been dead almost a year, and John still grieved for her. Whatever differences they'd had couldn't matter anymore.

John would always remember Caro as being young and beautiful, vibrant and alive. They'd fallen madly, passionately in love eight years ago and made a life together that was now unexpectedly and tragically over. Their love lived on, though. Not only in Gracie's person, but in John's heart.

To Leah's way of thinking, that was why her death had caused him such anguish. No marriage was perfect, and no two people ever agreed about everything. But John *had* loved Caro, and his love for her survived.

At least, that was what she wanted to believe—*needed* to believe, in all honesty. Otherwise, her eight-year, self-imposed exile would have been for nothing.

"Good morning, Aunt Leah. May I please, please, please have pancakes for breakfast?" Gracie asked as she came into the kitchen, her pace almost sprightly and her voice cheerful.

Drawn from her reverie, Leah noted that the little girl wasn't wearing her brace. Nor did she seem to be favoring her left leg the slightest bit, even after all the physical exercise she'd had the day before.

"Sure thing," she agreed. "I can add some blueberries or bananas to the batter, too. What sounds good to you?''

"Blueberries," John said as he, too, joined them.

"No, Daddy, bananas," Gracie demanded with a pretty pout.

"Okay, bananas it is." He ruffled his daughter's blond curls, then crossed to the coffeemaker, casting Leah a smiling glance as she began to assemble the necessary ingredients on the counter.

"You're such a pushover, John. Gracie likes blueberries, too," she teased, glad to see he was in a good mood again that day.

He looked rested, too, which meant he'd probably had a decent night's sleep—unlike her.

"What can I say?" he quipped back. "I'm a sucker for beautiful women, and I have two of the most beautiful women in the whole wide world right here with me. I bow to your wishes."

John made the courtly gesture with a grin, causing Gracie to giggle and Leah to shake her head in wry amusement.

"You're certainly full of yourself today," she said, ladling batter onto the hot griddle. "Not that I'm complaining. I like having someone bow to my wishes. It's such a rare occurrence."

"Gracie's getting her banana pancakes. You should have a wish granted, too, fair lady. So tell me please, what is your wish?" he asked.

Leah hesitated for several moments, considering the idea that immediately came to mind. There'd been something she'd wanted to do the past week, something she was certain Gracie would enjoy, too. She hadn't been sure how John would feel about it, though. Now that he'd opened the door, so to speak, she might as well tell him.

"What I'd really like is for you to take me and Gracie to see your lab at the university," she said, setting plates of banana pancakes in front of him and his daughter.

John met her gaze, his expression shifting from one of surprise to one of gratification in the space of a few moments.

"Oh, Daddy, can we? Can we *please* see your lab today?" Gracie pleaded. "I promise I won't touch anything."

"Me, neither," Leah chirped, relieved to see that John seemed pleased by the idea, though he hadn't actually agreed to it yet.

"Are you sure that's how you want to spend Sunday afternoon?" he asked, his twinkling eyes belying his solemn tone. "Being cooped up in a dreary old laboratory on a bright, sunny day doesn't sound like much fun to me."

"Positive," Leah replied.

"Yes, Daddy, positive," Gracie echoed.

"All right, then. The lab it is."

"Can we please, please, *please* look through a microscope and see stuff bubble in a big tube?" his daughter begged, her excitement and anticipation obvious.

"I imagine that can be arranged," John told her.

Leah wanted to hug him, her heart warmed by his uninhibited enthusiasm for the outing. Instead, she allowed herself only to give his arm an appreciative squeeze as she refilled his mug with coffee.

Quick as a flash he caught her hand in his before she could move away.

"So you really want to see my lab, huh?" he asked, his fingers tightening gently around hers.

"I'm a science teacher. I love laboratories of all sizes and shapes. I imagine yours will put my dinky workspace at St. Augusta's to shame, but that's okay. I still want to see it."

"A dinky lab, huh? That can't provide much of a challenge for you." He eyed her thoughtfully. "You know, you could always move back to Missoula permanently and come to work for me. We're state-of-the-art thanks to the grants I've received, and there's money available to hire an additional lab assistant. There's also room in our graduate-studies program for another student if you're interested in working on a master's degree."

John's pensive expression and grave tone made Leah's heart flutter. He was offering her something she could all too easily allow herself to want. She loved lab work and had always wanted to pursue a higher degree. She hadn't had an opportunity to do either in Chicago.

"Oh, cool, Aunt Leah," Gracie chimed in. "Then you could stay here with us forever and ever, and we could be a real family."

Frowning, Leah eased her hand from John's grasp. She didn't want either him or Gracie getting any ideas about the prolongation of her stay in Missoula. Working closely with John wouldn't be good for her emotionally in the long run. And there was no way they could ever be a real family.

"No can do," she advised them in as cheerful a voice as she could muster. "I have responsibilities in Chicago, you know."

"I think she means Kyle," Gracie whispered loudly to her father as Leah walked back to the counter.

"Oh, yeah, him," John whispered back conspiratorially, making Leah smile as she cleaned the griddle. "Not to worry, sweetie. She insists he's just a friend."

Leah wanted to protest, but she figured she'd be better off ignoring the issue of Kyle, the issue of moving back to Missoula and the issue of being a real family altogether. She didn't want to ruin their prospects for another pleasant day together.

"Come on, you two, finish your breakfast or we'll never get out of here," she instructed, instead.

To Leah's relief, both of them complied without any further mention of the subjects she most wanted to avoid discussing. But a glimpse of the look in John's eyes when he caught her gaze assured her that he had only retreated temporarily. There would be more probing about her past and prodding about her future plans to come from him, and she would be wise to brace herself for it.

Because the weather was close to perfect and Gracie seemed to be getting around quite well without her brace, they decided to walk the relatively short distance from John's house to the university campus. Cyclists, guys and girls on in-line skates, and other walkers were out in force as well, enjoying the fine day, tourists taking the place of students who'd returned to their hometowns until August and the start of the fall semester.

On the neatly trimmed lawn of the quadrangle, groups of young people lounged on blankets, talking, reading or listening to music while soaking up the sun. Several games of Frisbee were also in motion, some including leaping dogs of various sizes and shapes that made Gracie laugh with delight.

"I wish I could have a dog like that," she said, pointing to a tri-colored Australian shepherd that raced across the lawn, then jumped and spun in midair to catch a bright red disk.

"You'd have to spend a lot of time with him, teaching him how to behave first, then how to play with toys," John advised her. "You'd also have to make sure he had food and water and a clean, dry place to sleep."

"He could sleep on my bed, Daddy," she stated so decisively that both John and Leah laughed.

"Help me out here," he said to Leah.

"What your dad's trying to say is that having a dog is a lot of responsibility, Gracie. Are you ready to look after a pet and take care of it even if it means having less time to spend with your friends or read or watch television?" she asked the little girl.

"Sure," Gracie replied blithely.

"Okay, then, I'll think about it," John told her as they reached the building where his microbiology lab was located.

Glancing at Leah, he offered her a rueful smile, and she laughed again, sure he hadn't a clue what he'd gotten himself into. Her heart now set on having her own dog, Gracie was just strong-minded enough to pester the heck out of him until she got one. Of course he was such a pushover where his daughter was concerned that Leah was sure he'd cave in long before the summer was over.

It was cool and quiet inside the science building, although Leah noticed that the doors to several of the offices they passed were open and the lights were on. Other people were apparently working, also, despite it being a Sunday. John had probably been here working many a Sunday, too, but fortunately he didn't seem so inclined today.

They came to his laboratory eventually, and while it wasn't bustling with activity, the overhead fluorescent lights were on and four ambitious graduate students were busy peering into microscopes and jotting down notes or working diligently at the computers. They all greeted John with deference, then immediately went back to their tasks.

The lab was indeed state-of-the-art, Leah acknowledged, inhaling the indescribably sweet and organic smell of the chemicals and various culture media being used. While neither strong nor noxious, the odor was distinct and oh-so-familiar to her, reminding her of the many enjoyable hours she'd spent on lab projects of her own.

Four benches with dull-black countertops spread across almost the entire length of the room with narrow passages between them. Each bench was fitted with sinks and shelves to house flasks of various sizes. The most-often-used chemicals were readily available and easily accessible, too. There were also pointed metal cones to which the Bunsen burners could be connected by rubber hosing, electronic scales and centrifuges.

At one end of the room Leah also saw a hood—a tentlike structure with arm-length gloves in which to fit your hands to work with toxic materials. Desks skirting the walls of the lab held high-tech computers with huge screens. A very large refrigerator decorated with Far Side cartoons hummed in an alcove. Toward the very back of the room, separated by a half-windowed wall, was John's office.

"Wow," she breathed as she tried to take it all in without appearing too envious.

"I thought you'd like it," John said, making no effort to hide his well-deserved pride of place.

"'Like' doesn't even begin to describe how I feel," Leah admitted with a wry smile.

"Is this really where you work, Daddy?" Gracie asked, her awe equally apparent.

"Yes, it is, sweetie."

"It looks kind of scary to me." Her voice was grave.

"Some of the things we use here can be dangerous if we're not careful, but we're all trained to be very, very careful all the time."

"Can you show me how a microscope works?"

"Sure thing."

While Leah stayed quietly out of the way, John demonstrated the various items of equipment that filled his laboratory, starting with the high-powered microscopes that seemed to fascinate Gracie most. She was especially enthralled by the "wiggly stuff" she saw when she peered through the lens.

Watching father and daughter huddle together over a microscope warmed Leah's heart. Not only was their love for each other evident, but also the enjoyment they got from spending quality time together. John was a patient teacher and Gracie an eager, willing student. Leah could easily see that despite all they had lost when Caro died, they still had a very special bond. It had needed nothing more than a little nurturing.

"What about you, Aunt Leah? Do you want to look in the big microscope?" Gracie asked, happily drawing her into their sphere of activity again.

"Yes, please." Taking the little girl's place at the lab bench, she bent down, looked through the lens and immediately identified the specimen on the slide swimming with tiny creatures as pond water. "Interesting," she noted. "But it's not part of your current research project, is it?"

She cocked an eyebrow at John as she straightened again.

"No, it's not. We're actually in the process of identifying and describing a unique surface protein on the bacteria responsible for whooping cough, so a lot of our work has to be done under the hood."

"Can you make something bubble, Daddy?" Gracie asked.

From the graduate students came a collective snort of laughter that had John glaring in their direction and Leah smiling.

"Had a little unexpected chemical reaction recently?" she asked in a teasing tone.

"It happens to the best of us occasionally," he replied. Then to Gracie, as he positioned an empty flask well away from her on the lab bench and selected two simple nontoxic compounds from the array on hand, he said, "Watch this."

To the little girl's delight, he created a greenish-yellow foamy mess that gurgled as if with a life of its own.

"Oh, Daddy, that's so cool!" Gracie exclaimed, her eyes wide with excitement. "I want to work in a big laboratory just like you when I grow up. It's so fun, isn't it?"

"She's definitely your daughter," Leah quipped as Gracie turned her attention back to the microscope.

She'd intended her comment as a compliment. But instead of responding with fatherly pride as Leah had fully expected, John seemed to stiffen as he rinsed out the flask in the sink. His expression shifted subtly, as well, a shadow darkening his features. Then, just as suddenly, he regained some of his earlier equanimity.

"Most kids her age are fascinated by laboratories. By the time she's thirteen, she'll be more interested in clothes and boys and makeup."

"I wasn't," Leah pointed out.

"You were different."

"Not that different," she protested, wondering why he seemed so determined to disallow something about his daughter that should have pleased him.

"Gracie's more like her mother than me," he said in a tone that brooked no argument.

"In looks maybe, but otherwise—" Leah began, unwilling to let the matter drop.

"Gracie, would you like to see how the sleeves work under the hood?" he asked, cutting Leah off neatly without the slightest apology.

"Oh, yes, please," Gracie replied as he'd obviously known she would.

"You, too, Leah?"

He glanced at her but didn't meet her gaze, frustrating her all the more. Yet again she'd said the wrong thing to him, causing him to shut her out. But what had it been this time? Just an observation that Gracie was definitely his daughter. What could possibly have been wrong with that?

Another quandary about John to consider, she thought, aware that the list seemed to grow longer with every passing day.

"Leah?" he asked again with the barest hint of impatience.

"Yeah, sure, I'd like to see how they work," she answered at last as she joined him and Gracie in front of the hood.

Gracie was captivated with the magical sleeves, as well as the high-tech computers that were also included in John's tour of the laboratory. Leah trailed along behind them, her interest focused more on John and how he interacted with his daughter than on the various items of equipment.

She couldn't find any clues at all to his odd disavowal that Gracie had inherited his interest in scientific study. Why would he deny all the similarities Leah could so easily see that they shared? Why credit only Caro's genes as influencing the kind of young woman their daughter would eventually become? As they left the building and headed home across the campus quadrangle, bustling with even more activity now that it was late afternoon, she finally gave up grappling with her questions.

Though Gracie hadn't voiced any complaints, John had noticed that she seemed to be dragging a bit and had hoisted her onto his shoulders amidst much groaning on his part and giggling on hers. Leah kept pace beside them but made no effort at conversation. John didn't seem inclined to talk to her, either. So she contented herself with savoring the warmth of the sun on her face.

She wasn't paying much attention to the other people passing by on the sidewalk, so when someone called her name, she stopped in her tracks and looked up in surprise.

"I thought it was you," said the young woman with short, spiky auburn hair who halted in front of her, a baby in her backpack. Beside her stood a slightly older, bookish-looking man pushing a stroller that held a boy not much more than three years old.

"Susan Moore—or should I say Susan Moore-Tanner?" Leah exclaimed, smiling delightedly at the woman who had been one of her closest high-school friends. "How are you?"

"Busier than I thought I'd ever be," Susan replied with a wry smile of her own. "This is my husband,

Brett, and little Brett in the stroller, and my daughter, Janna.'' She gestured to the other members of her family. ''I'm really surprised to see you here. You should have called to tell me you're back in town. Have you finally decided that you *can* come home again?''

''I'm just visiting for the summer. Helping out an old friend, actually. It came up rather suddenly or I would have let you know ahead of time. I *have* been meaning to call you, but I've only been here about a week and I'm still getting settled in.'' She introduced John, whom Susan seemed to remember, and Gracie, with whom her toddler son seemed to be enchanted, then continued, ''How about you? Still glad you didn't move to Bozeman?''

''Oh, yes. I'm so glad Brett decided to move here, instead, to open a branch office of his father's insurance agency.'' Susan glanced at her husband and they exchanged loving smiles. Leah felt extremely envious.

''But, hey,'' Susan continued, meeting Leah's gaze again, ''why don't we catch up on our news over dinner one night this week? Tuesday, maybe?'' She glanced at Brett again and he nodded in agreement.

''Is it okay if I take off Tuesday night?'' Leah asked John. She wanted to be sure he'd be available to look after Gracie.

''No problem at all.''

''Tuesday night it is,'' Susan said, digging out a pen and paper from her fanny pack. ''Give me your telephone number in case I have a kid-related emergency, and John's address so I can pick you up.'' As Leah wrote down the information, Susan added, ''Debra's in town, too, visiting her mother, and Sarah still lives in the area. She has a flower shop down in Hamilton. I'll call them and see if they can join us, too.''

"That would be great," Leah said. "I'm so glad we ran into each other."

"I've really missed you, Leah. But it's been such fun getting postcards from all the exotic places you've traveled and your long, newsy letters at Christmas. You lead such an exciting life and you seem so happy in Chicago."

"And here I've been thinking you're the one living the good life," Leah admitted, eyeing Susan's children with a pang of longing.

"You don't know the half of it," Susan assured her, laughing. "See you Tuesday night."

"I'm looking forward to it."

As Susan headed off with her family and she and John continued on their own way home, Leah risked a quick glance at him.

"Are you sure you don't mind my taking a night off?" she asked.

"I don't know, Leah. Now that I think about it, you want to take one night off after more than a week of being on duty twenty-four/seven? That does seem a little excessive, especially considering the exorbitant salary I'm paying you," he grumbled. There was a distinctive twinkle in his eyes.

"Well, sir, I suppose you could dock my wages," she replied.

"Not this time, but I'd prefer you didn't make a habit of carousing with your wild-and-crazy friends on too regular a basis. I'm responsible for you while you're living in my house, you know. I wouldn't want to have to explain to Cameron and Georgette how I had to bail you out of jail."

"Like that would ever happen. In case you've forgotten, Susan, Debra, Sarah and I were four of the dullest, most boring girls ever to graduate from Hellgate High.''

"Yeah, but you're all grown up now, and you especially have become quite worldly-wise.''

"Don't worry, John, I'll be a perfect lady Tuesday night. You will not have to bail me out of jail. I promise.''

Happier by the minute about running into one of her old friends, Leah found herself looking forward to Tuesday night rather excitedly as they walked on down the sidewalk. She had planned to contact Susan and the others who'd been part of their high-school crowd, but the timing hadn't seemed right while John was still resentful of her presence in his house. Now that they had established a friendlier relationship, she didn't mind taking some time off for herself.

In fact, Leah knew it was a good idea for her to start going out, not only with friends, but also on her own. It would also be healthy for John and Gracie to spend more time on their own together, just as it would be healthy for her to have other things and especially other people to think about.

She had allowed John to occupy her mind, as well as her time, more completely than she should have the past week. Unless she made an effort to maintain some of the independence she'd worked so hard to attain the past eight years, she would be miserable when she returned to Chicago at the end of the summer. Having as good a time as possible on Tuesday night was a start in the right direction, one she now knew that she had to make for her own well-being.

Chapter Nine

John knew he should go upstairs to bed even though there was no chance he'd be able to sleep. Pacing through the first floor of his house Tuesday night, or rather, very early Wednesday morning, wasn't doing him the slightest bit of good. And it most certainly hadn't worked the kind of magic that seemed necessary to bring Leah home again.

For the umpteenth time since midnight, he wondered what she, Susan, Debra and Sarah could possibly be doing in Missoula, Montana, at what was now almost two in the morning. Most of the restaurants closed by ten, leaving only a handful of local bars as late-night hangouts. And some of those, many, in fact, could get awfully rough and rowdy after midnight. Surely the four friends hadn't ended up at any of them.

But what business was it of his if they had? They were adults, after all, and if they didn't have the sense to stay

out of places that could be dangerous, they would have
to deal with whatever trouble they ran into on their own.

John didn't want Leah running into any trouble,
though. He didn't want anything harmful to happen to
her anywhere at any time. He hadn't been kidding on
Sunday when he'd said he felt duty-bound to look out
for her well-being; the part about bailing her out of jail,
yes, but not the part about responsibility. Yet he had no
right to dictate what she could and couldn't do, nor with
whom.

Not that he wanted to have that kind of power over
her.

Cursing under his breath, John crossed the kitchen,
flung open the refrigerator door and grabbed another
beer. He didn't know what he wanted anymore where
Leah was concerned. Or maybe, if he was inclined to be
totally honest with himself for a change, he would finally
admit that he knew exactly what he wanted, and he was
frustrated as hell by the fact that he couldn't see any
way to ever have it.

She had been living in his house less than two weeks,
and determined as he'd originally been to keep some
distance between them, he'd already failed miserably.
Effortlessly, Leah had drawn him into the circle she'd
created with her warmth and radiance, making him feel
like a part of the patched-together family she'd known
instinctively he and Gracie needed.

He looked forward to the meals they shared mornings
and evenings, and the outings they invariably took together, as much as Gracie did. Leah gave him legitimate
reasons to spend time with her and his daughter, and he
could no more turn his back on those golden opportu-
nities now than he could fly to the moon.

But every time he caught himself enjoying the time

he spent with Leah and Gracie, he also experienced a gut-wrenching sense of guilt. What right did he have to savor the good things life now offered him when Caro was dead and buried because of his selfish, stubborn behavior? More important, what right did he have trying to think of ways to make Leah a permanent part of his life when he could never be completely honest with her about just how reprehensible his behavior toward Caro had been?

Striding through the house to one of the front windows, John thought back to the offer he'd made Leah at the lab on Sunday afternoon. He hadn't been lying when he said he could hire another assistant, nor when he told her there was an opening for another graduate student in the microbiology program and he could easily see that it was hers if she wanted it.

He still couldn't understand what had come over him to make such an offer except maybe the sudden vision he'd had of them not only living together, but also working together, sharing their lives to the fullest as he had never been able to do with Caro.

Staring out at the dark, deserted street, John knew he should be relieved that Leah hadn't seemed to take him seriously. He wasn't sure what he would have done or how he would have felt if she'd immediately agreed to his offer or if she'd brought it up later to discuss in more detail.

No, that wasn't true, he admitted with a rueful twist of his lips. He would have been happier than he'd been in more years than he cared to count. But he would also have been overwhelmed by very real and undeniable doubts about where, exactly, their relationship would—not to mention *could*—end up going.

Not much farther than it had already without a great

deal more honesty on his part about the past. And with that depth of honesty he would surely lose whatever respect Leah now had for him, along with any love she might have been able to find for him in her heart.

If he had to settle for her friendship only, rather than let her find out the truth about him, then he would. It was better than losing her altogether. In fact, anything was better than that. Gracie needed her too much, and in all truthfulness, so did he. He had already robbed his daughter of the most important person in her life. He would never knowingly say or do anything to rob her of anyone else she loved as much as she obviously loved her aunt Leah.

Thinking of Gracie, John remembered Leah's comment about how like him the little girl seemed to be when they were together in the lab on Sunday. More than anything, he'd wanted to believe the truth of her words. Yet Caro's angry statements the night she'd died echoed in his mind, belying the possibility. Hard as it was for him to admit that Caro had been telling the truth about Gracie, neither could he accept that she would have hurled such a hateful, hurtful lie at him.

Outside, headlights beamed through the darkness and the distinctive low hum of an idling engine came from the direction of the driveway, dragging John's attention back to the moment. About time, too, he thought, glancing at his watch, his relief almost palpable. He couldn't wait to hear what the four women had been up to until two-thirty in the morning.

He stayed by the window in the darkened living room, listening as Leah and Susan exchanged high-spirited good-night wishes. Leah took her time walking up the sidewalk to the front door, fitting her key into the lock and letting herself into the house.

Get FREE BOOKS and a FREE GIFT when you play the...

LAS VEGAS GAME

Just scratch off the gold box with a coin. Then check below to see the gifts you get!

YES! I have scratched off the gold Box. Please send me my **2 FREE BOOKS** and **gift for which I qualify.** I understand that I am under no obligation to purchase any books as explained on the back of this card.

335 SDL DUYG   235 SDL DUYW

FIRST NAME   LAST NAME

ADDRESS

APT.#   CITY

STATE/PROV.   ZIP/POSTAL CODE

(S-SE-03/03)

◄ DETACH AND MAIL CARD TODAY! ►

John finished the last swallow of his beer and waited expectantly until she'd shut and locked the door again.

"Have fun?" he asked, noting as he had earlier when she'd first left the house for her night out, how well her short, narrow denim skirt showed off her legs. She wore a red tank top, too, but had slipped on the short denim jacket that matched her skirt to ward off the chill of night.

Visibly startled by his presence in the living room, Leah spun around in the entryway and stared at him, her eyes wide. He sauntered toward her, glad to see that she looked none the worse for wear. Her dark hair was a little more tossed and tangled than it needed to be, especially since it made her look sexy as hell. But that was probably a result of riding in the car with the windows rolled down, something he remembered she'd always loved to do on a summer night.

"John…you're still up?" She sounded surprised and somewhat dismayed as she offered him a tentative smile.

"Still up, as you can see," he acknowledged, his tone sounding to his ears slightly more sarcastic than he'd intended. "And waiting for an answer. Did…you… have…fun?"

"Lots of fun," she replied matter-of-factly, her smile fading. "Thanks for asking." Turning away, she headed for the hallway that led to the kitchen, den and ultimately her room. "See you in the morning."

"It's morning already," he pointed out as he followed her, empty beer bottle in hand. He had to throw it in the recycling bin, didn't he? "You girls close down a bar somewhere or what?"

In the dimly lit kitchen Leah paused and faced him again. Something about the look on her face should have warned him he was close to overstepping a boundary, but he was a beer or two less cautious than he should have been. She gazed at him steadily, her eyes clear and questioning, and one corner of her mouth, her full-lipped, luscious mouth, curved up in a challenging way.

"We're not girls, we're adult women," she said. "And although it's none of your business, we did not close down a bar. We closed down a honky-tonk dance hall in Hamilton. Then we went to Sarah's house for pie and coffee, then Susan, Debra and I drove back to Missoula."

Casually she slipped off her jacket and hung it over a kitchen chair. Though she still looked at him, his attention was diverted by the red tank top. It seemed molded to her firm, full breasts, showing off her pouting nipples while also revealing the smooth, bare skin of her arms, now lightly tanned by the sun.

"I wasn't aware you frequented honky-tonk dance halls or that you even danced, for that matter," he muttered, his mouth suddenly gone dry.

"To be honest, I'm *not* in the habit of going to dance halls. But it sounded like fun when Sarah suggested it. It was, too, and I only danced to the slow songs."

Leah's smile was much too smug, much too…self-satisfied by several degrees for John's peace of mind.

"Meet anyone interesting?" he couldn't help but ask.

"Not really."

"In any case, it's kind of late to be gallivanting around, isn't it?" he asked as he passed close by her to dispose of his bottle in the bin stashed in the pantry.

"I wasn't aware I had a curfew or that gallivanting around wasn't allowed." Her tone had changed again to one most definitely laced with amusement.

John knew that he should go along with her humorous attitude, make some silly, self-deprecating remark and take himself off to bed. But the beer had removed more than a little of his natural inhibition, and that in turn had him behaving recklessly.

Somewhere in the back of his mind he realized that in the light of day he would be sorry. Just then, though, he didn't really care. He wanted something from Leah, some acknowledgment of the worry she'd caused him and her regret.

"You don't have a curfew, but while you're living in my house, under my protection, I expect you to behave responsibly."

She responded by laughing in a low and musical way that shot right through him, making his pulse pound with desire. In her close-fitting top and short skirt, her head tipped back and her dark hair rippling around her shoulders, she looked so invitingly touchable that he grabbed hold of the back of one of the kitchen chairs in an attempt to maintain at least some semblance of self-control.

Then she met his gaze, her eyes twinkling merrily, and said, "Oh, John, you sound just like a nineteenth-century patriarch chastising the wayward hired help. I'm a twenty-first-century, independent woman. I'm the only one responsible for me no matter where I live or what I do. There's no need for you to worry about me."

"You're wrong, Leah. There's every need," he growled, his attempt at holding back instantly rendered futile.

He took the few steps necessary to close the distance separating them, put his hands on her arms, and then, instead of giving her the common sense-inducing shake she deserved, he bent his head, claimed her mouth with his and kissed her long and hard.

She tensed for a few seconds, her shoulders squaring

under the gentle grasp of his hands. But as his kiss deepened, becoming more demanding, she uttered a quiet sigh and melted against him in sensual surrender.

Opening her mouth, she welcomed without further hesitation the masterly, all-consuming and darkly compelling sweep of his tongue. Her hands gripped his waist, then moved up to press against his back, urging his body closer to hers. She angled her head to allow him easier access and fit herself to him, her softness cupping the sudden, blood-pounding hardness of him as if two missing puzzle pieces had finally been fitted together with ultimate perfection.

Only when her hands roved down the length of his back again to tug the hem of his T-shirt free of his jeans, then slipped under to caress his bare skin, did he finally regain his senses.

Breaking off their kiss as suddenly as he'd initiated it, John raised his head, took a step back and, grasping Leah firmly by the wrists, drew her hands away from him. She stared at him wide-eyed for a few moments, her mouth slightly open and glistening. Her breathing had become quick and shallow, as if she'd been running.

She blinked finally, took in a steadying gulp of air and seemed to give herself a mental shake. Then her expression turned to one of confusion. She eyed him a few seconds longer, then started to speak, but he immediately cut her off.

"I'm sorry, Leah. I shouldn't have done that. More importantly, I shouldn't have questioned you the way I did. You're right. You're an independent woman. But it was late. I couldn't sleep and I was worried about you," he explained, looking past her to avoid meeting her questioning gaze.

Letting go of her wrists, he took another step back, increasing the distance between them once more.

"I don't think you kissed me the way you did because you were worried about me," she said, her voice soft and a little shaky as she rubbed the fingers of her right hand against the skin of her left wrist for a moment.

Then, reaching out, she touched his face with her fingertips in such a way that he knew she expected him to focus his full attention on her.

"Kissing you was a mistake," he repeated firmly. "I don't know why I did it. I just know I shouldn't have. I don't want you getting any false ideas...."

In fact, he didn't want to be tempted into getting any ideas himself, he realized. And the best way to guarantee that wouldn't happen was to put Leah off as pragmatically as possible, even if it meant hurting her feelings.

"You don't want me to get any false ideas?" she asked, her tone shifting to contain an obvious element of anger. "False ideas about what, John? That you care about me?"

"Of course I care about you, Leah. You've been a good friend to me and you've been wonderful with Gracie."

"You don't kiss a good friend the way you kissed me, John Bennett, and you know it." Her anger was even more apparent and now also edged with bewilderment.

"I know, and I'm sorry about that. I admit I got a little carried away. It's been a while since I...well, you know, and I let certain physical needs get away from me when I shouldn't have, and I'm really sorry, Leah. It's not my intention to use you—"

"Nor mine to allow myself to be used to service your needs," she replied, taking a turn at cutting *him* off as she spun on her heel, grabbed her jacket and headed for the den.

"I'm really sorry," he said again.

"Apology accepted." She paused in the doorway and looked back at him, her eyes glittering in a way that made him think she might be about to cry. "I plan to sleep in tomorrow morning. Can you look after Gracie until ten o'clock?"

"I can take her to the lab with me and bring her back at lunchtime. How would that be?"

Even in the dimly lit kitchen, John could see not only the hurt and confusion in Leah's expression, but also the sudden weary slump of her shoulders. Knowing that he'd done that to her, that he'd spoiled what had been an enjoyable evening for her, made him feel more remorseful than ever.

"That would be fine," she replied quietly.

As Leah turned away again, John had to stop himself from going after her. He would only make bad matters worse, *could* only make bad matters worse. Better to let her believe the feelings she'd so accurately sensed in the kiss they'd shared weren't real, after all. Better to let her think he had held her close only out of a need for physical release, not out of the love he so truly felt for her, but couldn't allow himself to act upon.

Much as he hated seeing her hurt by his actions, it wasn't as bad as leading her on would have been. He couldn't offer her the honesty she deserved, not the complete and utter honesty of a revealed past that had to be the foundation of any future he hoped to share with her. Anything less than that would stand between them always as any other kind of lie would, insidiously eating away at any bond he tried to form with her.

Trudging upstairs, John felt his whole body ache with

a wanting he would never be able to assuage. How he wished he could change the past. How he wanted to go back eight years, to choose rightly, instead of wrongly.

But then, would he have had Gracie in his life? He wouldn't trade her for anything, and so had to live with the choices he'd made and allow Leah to find the happiness she deserved with someone more worthy of her than he could ever be.

Chapter Ten

Somehow Leah made it into her room. Somehow she managed to shut the door and toss her jacket on the bed and kick off her loafers, all in an angry daze undermined by a sense of loss and confusion. She knew she shouldn't try to make rhyme or reason of John's behavior in her befuddled state. But she couldn't just crawl into bed, put it out of her mind completely and instantly fall asleep, either. She had to try to figure out how much of what he'd said, what he'd done, had been based on honest emotion and how much to discount as a retreat from those same feelings.

She had accused him of impersonating a Victorian patriarch, but it had also been endearing to know that he'd been concerned enough about her well-being to pace the floor, waiting for her to come home. She'd been honestly annoyed, though, that he'd felt entitled not only to question her judgment, but also to comment on it in a derogatory manner.

She wasn't a silly little twit. She was an adult, and quite accustomed to looking out for herself in a major metropolitan area much larger and more dangerous than Missoula, Montana. Yet John had given her no credit at all for the experience and independence she'd worked so hard to attain.

Then he had kissed her in such a totally and completely unexpected way that the ground had shifted under her feet. With that one disconcertingly impulsive act, he had rocked her safe little world, belying everything she had schooled herself to believe about her emotional attachment to him—not to mention his emotional attachment to her—and the impossibility of their ever being able to share a future.

Just as suddenly, though, John had let go of her like the handle of a hot skillet pulled from an oven. The look on his face had held such utter dismay that her world had shifted yet again, leaving her no choice but to wonder what was real and what was only a figment of her imagination.

Sitting alone in her room, Leah knew she hadn't fantasized the deeply possessive demand of John's kiss. While she was far from being a sexually experienced woman, she did understand the difference between a casual encounter with someone of the opposite sex and an encounter highly charged with mutual desire.

He'd held her firmly yet gently, offering her no hope of resistance even if she'd wanted it, and his mouth had ravaged hers with a thoroughness that had stolen her breath away completely. He hadn't tensed when she'd explored the muscular contours of his back with her hands, either. Instead, he'd relaxed under her tender touch with an audible sigh. She knew enough about male anatomy, as well, to realize that the hard pressure against her softness had involved quite a bit more than the metal zipper of his jeans.

She had no doubt that John had wanted more from her in those long, shared moments of their kiss. And he hadn't been shy about letting her know it as he'd molded his body to hers. But when she'd clearly signaled her own readiness to take the next step in their mating dance, when she'd tugged his T-shirt free of his jeans and stroked his hot, bare skin with her seeking fingertips, then he'd suddenly, unbelievably changed course.

Perched on the side of her bed, rubbing her palms up and down her arms in an attempt to ward off the chill seeping into her bones, Leah remembered how decisively John had ended not only their kiss, but their entire romantic interlude. She had been momentarily disconcerted by his abrupt and unanticipated behavior. Then when he'd started making excuses, followed by apologies, anger had surged through her.

She'd wanted to rage at him indignantly, to accuse him of being a heartless tease. But somehow she'd managed to hang on to her composure. A mistake, he'd said as he backed away from her. Kissing her had been a mistake, one he wished he hadn't made because he didn't want her getting the wrong idea.

He'd explained away the sensuality of their kiss, as well, saying he'd obviously gotten a little carried away, but only as a result of the long period of celibacy he'd endured since Caro's death.

Long story short, he'd had *needs,* and she'd been handy. He'd lost control for a few moments and then, thank heavens, regained it again before he could do anything even more regrettable than merely kissing her.

Unexpectedly Leah's eyes filled with tears sparked by a belated, but now overwhelming, sense of humiliation. She'd been so sure that John had initiated their kiss out of honest love and desire for her and her alone. He'd been worried about her long absence, and when she'd teased him about it, he had wanted to prove to her that his feelings were no laughing matter. Or so she'd foolishly and regrettably assumed until he'd so indelicately apprised her otherwise.

Now it seemed she had no choice but to accept his explanation. Their close proximity in the dimly lit kitchen coupled with their voluble verbal exchange had merely been the catalyst for John's sexual reawakening. It hadn't had anything to do with her personally. She'd simply been a convenient means to an end. Any other woman would have served his purpose just as well.

He'd all but said as much, hadn't he? And who was she not to believe him? She'd never been the focus of his sexual desire. Caro had always had that honor. She'd always been only his pal, his buddy, his good friend, and now she was also his daughter's nanny.

Living in his home as she must for Gracie's sake, she was more available to him physically than she'd ever been. But she was also more available physically than any other woman. And John had made it clear that he wasn't going to treat her with disrespect. While he could take advantage of her close proximity to service his needs, he wouldn't.

She knew she ought to be grateful for his honesty, Leah thought, sniffling as she swiped at the tears, leaving damp patches on her face. He could have led her on so easily, then sent her back to Chicago at summer's end. And she would have willingly gone, stepping aside again.

At least now she knew how imperative it was for her to guard her emotions in the weeks ahead. She had denied the possibility of ever having a future with John for such a long time that it wouldn't be all that difficult to continue in the same vein. She would just have to remind herself on a regular basis they were only good friends, and that was all they would ever be to each other.

She was also going to have to pretend that their little exchange in the dimly lit kitchen had never taken place, she admitted as she finally stripped off her tank top and denim skirt and pulled a simple white cotton nightgown over her head. Otherwise it would be too painful to be in the same house with John, much less in the same room as they often were. She didn't want to spend the balance of the summer attempting to find ways to avoid his company. Nor did she want to have to hide out in her room every time there was a possibility of being alone with him.

Leah's mission had been—and would remain—creating as much of a family atmosphere as possible for Gracie, and she had really only just begun to make a success of it. Gracie was an intelligent little girl. She would be aware of any additional tension or any histrionics going on in the house between her and John, and it would upset her even more if John started staying away again as a result.

Gracie so obviously needed her father's company, and vice versa, that Leah vowed not to allow her own bruised emotions to interfere in any way with the special bond they'd begun to share lately. She was an adult, as she'd so succinctly pointed out to John. Her wants and needs had to be secondary to those of his six-year-old daughter. That was why she'd returned to Missoula in the first place, and that was why she would stay, regardless of any hurt she might suffer as a result.

Leah slept fitfully at first, her mind still whirling too furiously to allow her to do more than doze and wake, then doze and wake again. Finally, however, somewhere near dawn, she was so completely exhausted that she slept soundly and dreamed only fleetingly, if at all.

She didn't hear John and Gracie in the kitchen. In fact, she heard nothing until almost ten o'clock when the chatter of a squirrel in the tree outside her window brought her to a muddled wakefulness at last. She gazed at the clock on her nightstand and groaned softly, wondering how she was ever going to be able to pull herself together presentably by the time John brought Gracie home for lunch. She hadn't had enough to drink the night before to have a hangover, but her head ached and her eyes felt gritty as a result of all the crying she'd done, and her hair smelled of cigarette smoke from the dance hall.

She knew that a shower and shampoo, along with several cups of strong coffee, would help a lot. But Leah wanted to be more than just neat and clean and relatively wide-awake when she saw John again. As a matter of pride, she wanted to be cheerful and alert, her hair shimmering around her shoulders and all trace of the miserable hours she'd spent trying to sleep erased from her face. And that, she acknowledged, eyeing herself in the bathroom mirror, was going to take some doing.

By the time John and Gracie arrived at the house— he seeming rather subdued and she in high spirits—Leah was sure that she looked none the worse for wear. The hot shower and shampoo had helped enormously, as had the freshly brewed coffee and the bowl of fruit and yogurt she'd wisely forced herself to eat. She'd styled her

hair in a carefree tumble of curls and applied just enough
makeup to hide the dark circles under her eyes and give
her pale skin a coppery glow. She'd dressed modestly,
too, in comfortable khaki pants and a plain, white, loose-
fitting T-shirt.

She'd also made an effort with the luncheon prepa-
rations, fixing deli-style sandwiches with ham, Swiss
cheese, lettuce and tomatoes, on thick slices of whole-
wheat bread spread with Dijon mustard. She'd set out a
bowl of corn chips and another of sliced strawberries
and bananas, and had just finished arranging shortbread
and chocolate-chip cookies on a dessert plate when they
joined her in the kitchen.

"Hey, guys," she greeted them cheerfully. "I hope
you're hungry."

"Starving, Aunt Leah," Gracie answered dramatically
as she walked over to the sink to wash her hands.

"You didn't have to go to all this trouble," John said
as he, too, crossed to the sink.

"It wasn't any trouble at all," Leah assured him,
flashing a brilliant smile as she glanced in his direction.
Carefully, though, she avoided actually meeting his gaze
before she walked to the table and set down the plate of
cookies. "What would you two like to drink?"

"Milk," Gracie replied, slipping onto her chair.

Once again she had gone without her brace, and her
steps were surefooted and lively even after several hours.

"I'll get the drinks," John said. "There's no need for
you to wait on us."

"No, no...." Leah waved her hand with a dismissive
air. "You sit down and eat. You worked all morning
while I just lazed around in bed. Tea for you, John, or
would you rather have milk, too?"

As she attempted to breeze past him, he caught her

by the arm and gently turned her so that she had to face him. The touch of his hand, warm and dry against her bare skin, sent an electric shock through her body. Her senses on high alert, she made the mistake of meeting his gaze. His questioning look was intensely intimate as he stepped closer to her and lowered his voice for her ears only.

"Are you okay?" he muttered, his thumb rubbing rhythmically along the inside of her wrist.

Drawing from some deep inner reserve of strength she hadn't known she possessed, Leah made herself smile up at him reassuringly as she answered softly, "I'm fine, John, just fine. It was so good of you to let me sleep in." Then to Gracie as she freed herself from his hold, "Did you have fun at the lab with your dad this morning?"

With obvious reluctance John joined his daughter at the table while Leah poured milk for Gracie and tea for him, since he hadn't indicated another preference. But as Gracie elaborated on her morning adventure, he didn't immediately start to eat. Instead, he continued to watch Leah with a concentration that unnerved her.

Was he expecting her to fall apart? If so, she thought, he was going to be disappointed. She wasn't about to give him the pleasure of knowing his behavior toward her in the early hours of the morning had affected her in any way, good, bad or indifferent. He hadn't wanted her to get any false ideas, and she was going to make certain he saw for himself that she hadn't.

"Aren't you going to eat, too?" he asked when Gracie paused to gulp down a swallow of her milk.

"I ate something about an hour ago. You go ahead."

John finally took a bite of his sandwich, and after pouring one last cup of coffee for herself, Leah finally sat at the table, too, and even chose a chocolate-chip cookie to nibble on.

Gracie had evidently enjoyed spending the morning with her father. In a good mood, she agreed readily enough when Leah suggested they start work on some of the assignments the school had sent over to help get the little girl ready to join her first-grade class in September.

"Then can I play with Tiffany for a while?" she asked.

"If it's all right with her mother."

Turning her attention back to John as he finished his sandwich, Leah asked if he was going back to the lab.

"Yes, I have some work to do. But I'll be home for dinner. Let's plan to go out, okay?"

"Me, too, Daddy?"

"Of course, you, too, sweetie."

He continued to eye Leah hopefully, waiting for her agreement.

"Sure, sounds good to me," she said at last.

She'd wanted to tell him to take Gracie out on his own, to let her stay home alone. But to do what? Brood still more over his treatment of her earlier that morning?

No, she'd done enough of that already, and like a mathematician who'd taken the necessary steps to solve an equation, she'd come to her own conclusions about John's behavior the night before.

Worry about her had obviously lowered his guard, and as a result, his sense of relief at her safe arrival home hadn't been hindered by his normal reserve. Nor had his bantering with her, which had then taken a sexual turn, heightened by his loneliness since Caro's death. She, being available, had been a handy source of release, nothing more.

"You girls decide where you'd like to go, then," John said. "I'll be home by six."

"Zia's," Gracie stated decisively.

"Leah?" John eyed her questioningly.

"Zia's it is," she agreed.

"Can I call Tiffany now?" Gracie asked, scooting off her chair.

"Yes, but you have to do some schoolwork before you can play. Tell her she can come over at three o'clock, okay?"

"Okay, Aunt Leah."

As the little girl skipped into the den to use the telephone there, Leah stood and began to gather the empty plates. John sat back in his chair, one hand toying with his glass of tea. She could feel him watching her, could sense the overt assessment in his gaze as the silence stretched between them uncomfortably, at least for her.

She wished he would hurry off to the lab as he'd done during her first few days in his house. But he seemed all too content to stay in the kitchen with her, eyeing her with an unnerving contemplation she couldn't even begin to fathom.

So intent was she on scooping the leftover sliced fruit into a plastic container to store in the refrigerator that Leah didn't realize John had come to stand behind her at the counter until he spoke her name, his voice low, his breath tickling her shoulder. She whipped around to face him—her first mistake—then met his searching gaze.

He was so close to her she could feel the heat radiating off his body. That, coupled with the look in his eyes, a look that seemed to mirror the combination of desire and confusion she was feeling, made her insides melt into mush.

"Leah," he said, his voice softer still, an audible caress. "About what happened…" He paused, swallowed, looked away. "I said some things…"

"Don't worry, John, I understand completely," she assured him, hoping desperately to keep him from verbalizing yet again what a mistake he'd made by kissing her.

"No, I don't think you do." Reaching out, he gently touched her cheek. "I know I don't—"

"Tiffany's mom said Tiffany can come over to play at three-thirty. I hope it's okay that I said it's okay," Gracie announced with a giggle as she joined them in the kitchen again.

"That's great," Leah replied brightly, slipping past John to put the container of fruit in the refrigerator. "Now help me finish clearing the table so we can get to work on your school assignments."

She caught a glimpse of John's face and saw the frown creasing his forehead, but she was determined not to pay him any more attention.

That was easier said than done, however, Leah discovered as the day wore on. John left for the lab as she and Gracie finished tidying the kitchen, choosing to say no more to her in the little girl's presence. But Leah had the feeling he wasn't going to drop the subject of their passionate kiss completely. He had something more to say about it, something he seemed to believe she needed to hear.

Surely he'd said enough already, though. Surely he knew she wouldn't throw herself at him, that she wouldn't do anything to tempt him sexually, aware as she now was that any interest he might have in her was based solely on ease of access. She may have gotten a little carried away tugging at his T-shirt and touching his bare skin last night, but she had no problem whatsoever understanding and accepting the meaning of the word *no*.

Of course John just might want to recant some of what he'd said to her, Leah mused as the afternoon wore on and she had even more time to think once Gracie had successfully completed her schoolwork and Tiffany had come to play. But which of his off-putting remarks did he think she'd been dumb enough to misunderstand?

He'd said them all with such calm deliberation, the heat of any passion he'd allowed himself to feel already cooling rapidly as he refused to give her any false ideas. Well, he didn't have to worry. She'd assured him that she wasn't going to have any at all, at least where he was concerned—not ever.

By the time John returned home just before six o'clock and they left for dinner at Zia's, Leah had decided she'd done enough pondering for one day. She forced herself to relax and enjoy another respite from her nightly dinner duties. Not that she disliked cooking for John and Gracie, especially since they always helped with the cleanup, too. But it was nice to get out of the house for a couple of hours, even after being out the previous night.

The only problem with joining them on their outing was that she hadn't caught up on the sleep she'd missed staying up until the wee hours of the morning. The glass of red wine she'd ordered had her yawning long before she had finished her portabello-mushroom ravioli.

"I think we'd better get your aunt Leah home before she ends up with her face in her plate," John said as they spooned up the last of the spumoni ice cream they'd each ordered for dessert.

"Why would Aunt Leah put her face in her plate?" Gracie asked with a look of disbelief. "That would be so silly."

"Your father is afraid I'm going to nod off to sleep, and when I do, I won't be able to keep my head up," Leah explained, shooting John a wry smile. "And much as I hate to admit it, it *is* a possibility."

"It's still really early," Gracie pointed out. "Not even nine o'clock yet."

"Yes, but your aunt Leah was out very, very late last night. Or should I say until very, very early this morning?"

"What were you doing?" Gracie asked, wide-eyed.

"Visiting with some friends of mine I hadn't seen since I moved to Chicago, just like I told you," Leah replied, then added, "Imagine all the things you would have to talk about if you hadn't seen Tiffany for a long time."

"Like when we had our sleepover. Only *you* made us go to bed at ten o'clock."

"I think we'd better make sure your aunt Leah has an early night tonight herself," John said, taking some bills from his wallet to pay the waitress.

"I'm not arguing with that," Leah admitted with another yawn, then a self-conscious laugh.

Home again, Leah took herself off to bed before the clock could strike nine, much less ten, leaving John and Gracie to watch the animated movie he'd rented on his way home from the lab. It was about monsters who were afraid of children. Leah had seen it at the theater with Kyle and his younger son and had enjoyed it, as she knew John and Gracie would, too.

She didn't remember falling asleep. She must have done so as soon as her head hit the pillow. She'd opened the windows so she could enjoy the cool evening breeze, though, and it was the subtly intrusive sound of the blinds shifting and banging against the window sills that brought her slowly awake again.

The breeze had gone from cool to icy cold and now held a distinctive hint of dampness that normally presaged a rainstorm. It also blew up in gusts that rustled noisily through the trees.

As Leah sat up in her bed and glanced at the clock on her nightstand, noting it was almost two o'clock, a flash of lightning lit up the room. Almost immediately, a boom of thunder shook the house, making her wince.

The weather had been so fine since her arrival in Missoula, the sky so clear, the air so crisp and dry, that she'd forgotten about the sometimes violent summer storms that could blow up so suddenly. The lightning especially was dangerous, because it often sparked forest fires.

Another gust of wind came through the open windows, sending a shiver up Leah's spine as it carried with it the sharp patter of raindrops against the windows. She shoved her quilt aside, slipped out of bed and hurried over to shut the windows before the rain could dampen the carpet.

She also remembered leaving the kitchen window open when she'd retired for the night. She couldn't be sure that John had closed it before he went to bed, either, or that he would be woken by the storm and remember to do so now. Not wanting the wind and rain to do any damage, she hurried out of her room, across the den and into the kitchen, wearing only her long, sleeveless, white cotton nightgown.

The window was open, but luckily the rain was slant-

ing in another direction so the countertops hadn't gotten
wet as a result. She leaned over the sink and closed the
window, then tried to recall what other windows might
have been left open for the night.

The ones in Gracie's room, for sure, because the little
girl, too, liked the feel of the cool night breeze against
her face as she slept. Perhaps the ones in John's study
and his bedroom, as well. But if he happened to be so
sound asleep that he didn't awake and close those himself, he would have to suffer the consequences. She felt
uncomfortable enough breaching the privacy of the second floor to look in on Gracie and check his study, but
she wasn't about to venture into his bedroom, too.

As she padded through the house, rubbing her hands
up and down her arms to ward off the chill, another flash
of lightning split the darkness, followed more closely by
a crash of thunder. The patter of rain also became a
steady, unrelenting downpour.

Leah ran up the stairs, making her way instinctively
in the darkness. The door to John's study was open, the
room itself unoccupied. She crossed quickly to the windows and found them both firmly closed. She had just
turned to retrace her steps when she heard someone sobbing almost hysterically.

Gracie, Leah realized, her bare feet skimming over the
carpeted floor of the study. Down the hallway she flew
with her heart pounding. She had been so worried about
closing windows that she hadn't considered how frightening such a powerful storm might be for the little girl.

As she drew closer to Gracie's room, Leah heard the
rumble of John's voice as he tried to soothe his daughter,
though without any apparent success.

"I want Aunt Leah," Gracie cried. "Where's Aunt
Leah? I'm afraid for her, Daddy. The storm's going to

take her away just like it took my mommy away. It is, Daddy, it *is*."

"Leah's all right, Gracie," John tried to assure her. "She's downstairs, safe in her room, sound asleep."

"But I want her *here* with us, Daddy," Gracie sobbed uncontrollably.

"Oh, sweetie, I'm here," Leah said, moving swiftly across the room.

Dressed in sweatpants and a T-shirt, John sat on the edge of his daughter's bed, holding her close as she cried. Both he and Gracie looked up as she joined them, and they both looked equally relieved to see her. Gracie immediately freed herself from her father's hold, darted out of bed and across the room to fling herself into Leah's outstretched arms.

"I was so scared, Aunt Leah," the little girl whimpered softly as she clung to her. "So scared the storm would take you away just like it took my mommy away."

"I'm fine, Gracie, just fine," Leah assured her niece, lifting her into her arms and carrying her back to her bed, where John now stood uncertainly.

"You won't go, will you?" Gracie asked. "You, either, Daddy?"

"We'll both stay right here with you until the storm is over, okay?" John said, pulling the quilt back so that Leah could settle the little girl into her bed again.

Another flash of lightning lit up the room and more thunder made the windows, now closed, rattle ominously, but Gracie didn't flinch. Having Leah and her father right there with her was all it had taken to ease her fears. John tucked the quilt around his daughter's shoulders, then moved to the far side of the bed to sit down again, leaving Leah to sit on the near side, their loving presence forming a cocoon that gave the little girl a sense of safety.

As Gracie snuggled into her pillow with obvious contentment, John slid his arm along the top of the headboard and gave Leah's shoulder a gentle, grateful squeeze.

"Thanks," he murmured when she glanced at him in surprise.

"Storms are scary for me, too, sometimes," she acknowledged. "It's nice not to have to ride this one out all alone."

"Did you hear Gracie crying?"

"Only when I came upstairs to close the windows. The wind was actually what woke me."

Though the storm raged on, Leah saw that Gracie had closed her eyes. She would be asleep again soon, especially if they stayed with her until the worst of the weather had passed.

"I was just about ready to scoop Gracie up and come downstairs to your room," John said, his hand still gripping her shoulder warmly. "She's had trouble sleeping whenever the weather is bad, which is understandable. But she was really panicked about you tonight, hysterical almost. I just couldn't seem to convince her that you were safe in the house."

"Having me here the past few weeks must have brought memories of Caro closer to the surface of her consciousness. With the storm waking her, those memories were probably intensified in her mind, and what happened to Caro during one storm suddenly became what could happen to me in another. But I'm here and I'm safe, and I'm pretty sure Gracie's sleeping now."

Indeed, the little girl was breathing deeply and evenly, her mouth sketching a tiny, satisfied smile. How wonderful to be so easily calmed, to feel so completely secure just by having those you loved close at hand, Leah thought. But then, she felt much like her little niece, sitting there with John as the storm's strength finally began to diminish.

She was part of something here with them, something she hadn't dared hope to have for herself, at least not since her sad parting with Kyle. And really, she would be wise not to get her hopes up with John and Gracie, either. Her position here was only temporary, and she'd already been warned once about getting false ideas.

"Come on," he said, giving her shoulder another squeeze as he eased to his feet, careful not to disturb his daughter. "I'll walk you back to your room."

"I'm pretty sure I can find my own way," she replied with a teasing smile, standing, also.

"I wasn't insinuating that you couldn't," he returned mildly, his tone teasing, as well. "But I'm hungry and there's ice cream in the freezer and it's downstairs in the kitchen, close to your room."

"Oh, well, okay then…as long as you're not just being gallant."

"So now that I've been honest about my intentions at *your* instigation, I'm a self-serving jerk, huh?"

"No…"

She looked up at him as they walked down the hallways and smiled contritely.

John smiled back and slipped his arm around her shoulders. Companionably, she told herself, starting down the staircase with him. He was just being companionable. Still, her stomach quivered at the warmth and closeness they shared in the dark house, the rain now providing a steady but much more tranquil background tattoo against the roof and windows.

"Do you want to join me?" he asked, pausing to face her when they reached the kitchen.

"Not tonight." She tipped her head back and met his

gaze, then went very still as she saw the longing in his eyes.

His arm was still around her shoulders and it took only the slightest shift in his stance to bring her close enough to kiss. And kiss her he did, quite suddenly and without any seeming forethought, before she had a chance to back away or voice a protest.

Though Leah doubted she would have done either as she opened her mouth to the seeking stroke of his tongue. She simply sighed softly and slipped her arms around his waist, tasting him with an eagerness and lack of inhibition that matched his own.

He shifted his arm from around her shoulders, moving it down to her waist, using it to urge her closer, molding her body to his so that she could easily feel the evidence of his desire through the thin cotton of her nightgown. But unlike the last time he'd kissed her, Leah didn't allow herself to act on her own heightened desires.

She didn't arch against him as she so desperately wanted to do. She didn't tear at his T-shirt to caress his naked skin. She barely even allowed herself to breathe as the moments lengthened and their kiss deepened. She simply waited for the inevitable to happen, as it did so suddenly that it would have been surprising if she hadn't been expecting it all along.

"Jeez, Leah," John muttered, putting his hands on her shoulders as he broke off their kiss and backed away from her. "I—"

"I know," she interrupted so quietly that she amazed herself. "You're sorry—really sorry, in fact. You got carried away...physical needs...close proximity. Did I forget anything? Oh, yes, false ideas—I shouldn't get any of those." She took a step back and patted him reassuringly on the chest. "Don't worry, I won't."

"Leah." He sounded angry now.

But why, she didn't know, and she wasn't about to stay around long enough to find out, she vowed, shrugging off his hands and moving away from him, putting herself out of his reach.

"Honestly, John, we have to stop meeting like this. It does absolutely nothing for my self-esteem," she advised him with a breezy air. "Night-night."

She waved a hand at him and continued on to her room, forcing herself to maintain a measured pace despite her fear that he would follow her. Or was it hope...

Either way, he stayed in the kitchen, allowing her to reach the sanctuary of her room without anything further between them. She should have been relieved, she told herself as she curled up under her quilt and listened to the still-pattering raindrops. But her heart ached and her eyes filled with foolish tears.

She remembered how wanted, how *needed* she'd felt upstairs in Gracie's room. She'd been a part of something then, a part of something John created, and she'd been welcome there. But with John, alone in the kitchen, her status had changed dramatically.

She was worthy of his physical advances, but not his emotional commitment, and he was gentleman enough not to act on the one in the absence of the other. She knew she should be grateful for his attempts at honesty, as well as his honorable behavior.

Just then, though, alone in her bed, Leah found herself wishing he had set aside his emotional integrity and given in to his needs. She wouldn't get the wrong idea. She was too smart for that to happen. But at least for a few short weeks she could pretend she was more than just a friend to him.

Because she would have been more than that, if only temporarily, and that would have been better than nothing.

Chapter Eleven

John knew he'd screwed up royally where Leah was concerned. But in the days following the one-after-another exchanges they'd had in the kitchen, he could think of no way to make up for what he'd said and what he'd done.

Any excuses or apologies he considered offering were so lacking in truth they were ludicrous. There was no excuse for the way he'd behaved toward her, nor for the things he'd said. And while he was truly sorry for the hurt he'd so obviously caused her, he couldn't say he regretted kissing her—couldn't and wouldn't.

The closeness they'd shared during those moments, as short as they'd been, had held a vital essence so full of hope and the promise of dreams coming true that to deny it would be tantamount to denying life itself. Yet he couldn't allow himself to want for more of the same.

Not when the sins of his recent past, if revealed as they would have to be, would guarantee he'd never have it.

Leah didn't know what kind of man he really was— what kind of man he had become—in the years they'd been apart. And in her present position, just an old friend helping out by looking after his daughter, she didn't really need to know. He didn't like that his actions toward her twice already had caused her unnecessary pain and confusion. But that was nothing compared to the shock and horror she would surely feel if she ever found out the truth about those last moments he and Caro spent together before she drove off to her death.

At least that was what John tried to tell himself each time Leah refused to meet his gaze or, even worse, flashed a smile his way that didn't seem quite real because it didn't chase away the shadows in her eyes. To anyone else, including Gracie, she appeared happy enough. She even sounded happy enough most of the time. Her demeanor was just as pleasant as ever, perhaps even more so. But John knew her well enough to realize what an effort she had to be making.

Those kisses they'd shared, hungry kisses full of giving and taking in equal measure, had revealed to him not only the true depth of his desire for Leah, but also her desire for him. Her response to his greedy demands hadn't been casual or offhand in any way. She'd melted against him with a neediness that matched his own, and with a willingness to take matters several steps farther that had at first thrilled him, then pulled him up short just as quickly and surely as a splash of icy water in the face would have done.

He could so easily have been tempted to take Leah to bed, to savor the physical release she'd seemed to offer with such eagerness. He'd only been able to stop himself when the realization of how churlish that would have been had reared its admonishing head. He wanted more with Leah than a cursory affair, but having more required a degree of honesty that wouldn't, as far as he could see, benefit his cause at all.

To avoid further temptation John had gone back to spending longer hours at the lab the past couple of days. He still came home for dinner so he could spend time with Gracie and Leah, but then he'd go back to the university until the wee hours when he knew Leah was asleep. He'd intended to work at the lab on Saturday, as well. Only Gracie, firmly reminding him Friday night that the lawn needed mowing again, had kept him at home.

He'd busied himself with that chore until early afternoon, then set about completing several other odd jobs he'd let go for too long already. Leah had taken Gracie shopping at the local mall for some new clothes and shoes, so he hadn't had to worry about staying out of her way.

In fact, he had planned to be gone before they returned home. But by the time he'd showered, put on fresh shorts and a T-shirt and headed downstairs again to leave a note for them, he heard their light, laughing voices coming from the kitchen.

He was tempted to beat a hasty retreat to his study and hole up there for the remainder of the afternoon and evening, but then felt foolish for even considering such cowardly behavior. He had to find some middle ground that he could share comfortably with Leah, or he would make himself, Leah and especially Gracie miserable.

Leah had doggedly continued to try to provide a family framework of sorts for his daughter, and he couldn't do his part to hold that framework together if he hid out in his study or continued working long hours at the university on a regular basis.

"I see you had a successful expedition to the mall," he said, managing an upbeat tone as he joined them in the kitchen.

"More than you can imagine," Leah said, glancing his way with a cheery smile. She waved a hand at the brightly colored shopping bags stacked on the kitchen table and chairs. "Don't worry. I didn't spend all your money. Some of these things are mine."

"Well, that's a relief."

"Look, Daddy, look at what I got," Gracie demanded, pulling items from several of the bags. "Shorts and tops and a sundress and some new jeans and sandals and sneakers...."

"I thought you said you didn't spend all my money," John grumbled in a wry tone, directing a mock-stern look at Leah.

"All the stores were having really big sales, weren't they, Gracie?" Leah said as she separated her purchases from the purchases she'd made for his daughter.

John noted with disappointment that she didn't offer to show him her new clothes as Gracie had done. But then, he couldn't really expect her to, could he? His behavior had been too standoffish lately for her to feel comfortable sharing much of anything with him.

"Really *big* sales, Daddy. We saw Tiffany and her mom at one of the stores. They had almost as many packages as we did."

"Almost, huh?" John ruffled the little girl's hair, pleased she'd had so much fun shopping with Leah.

"Tiffany's mom said I could come over to their house for dinner, and I could spend the night, too. But Aunt Leah said we had to be sure it was okay with you first.

So is it, Daddy? Is it okay if I have dinner and spend the night at Tiffany's house?''

"Well, yes, I suppose so."

He glanced at Leah to see how she felt about the idea, but she seemed preoccupied with thoughts of her own. He wondered if she realized, as he did, that they would be alone together in the house tonight if Gracie stayed with Tiffany. And he wondered if her heart beat a little faster at the thought of the opportunity they'd have under those circumstances to explore their own personal relationship.

But he couldn't take advantage of that opportunity, could he? Couldn't and wouldn't, he vowed, as Leah must surely be aware.

"Oh, goodie, goodie!" Gracie jumped up and down and clapped her hands.

"I'll call Tiffany's mother and give her the good news," Leah said with a wry smile. "You take your clothes and shoes up to your room and put them away, then gather up what you want to take with you to Tiffany's and pack it in your backpack, okay?"

"Okay, Aunt Leah."

"I can take her over to Tiffany's house," John offered.

"I don't mind doing it," Leah said as she gathered her own packages off the table.

"No, really—"

"I insist—"

"You can both take me to Tiffany's house," Gracie decided. "Then you can go out on a date together."

John's gaze clashed with Leah's above his daughter's head, and he saw in her eyes an echo of the same dismay that had stabbed through him at the little girl's pronouncement. Was she also experiencing a sense of regret that they couldn't enjoy an evening out alone together because of the damage his recent conduct had done to their once-companionable relationship? He knew he certainly was.

"What a lovely idea," Leah murmured noncommittally, clutching several shopping bags in her hands.

"So you'll both take me to Tiffany's house?" Gracie asked.

"Yes, of course," John said.

"Then you'll go on a date?"

"That depends on your aunt Leah. She might have other plans for tonight."

As safe a thing as he could say, John figured, since Leah had gone off to her room and couldn't immediately disagree. And maybe they could at least have dinner somewhere, especially if he could make her understand that it was in her best interests for them to remain just friends in the weeks they had left together.

"I don't think she does, Daddy," Gracie replied as she skipped off to her room, her arms laden with her packages.

They drove the relatively short distance to Tiffany's house, Leah sitting beside him in the passenger seat of the Jeep and Gracie securely belted into one of the back seats. Gracie chattered away, excited about her first sleepover at her best friend's house since the accident. Completely free of the brace now, she could get around without any problems, and her exuberance was clearly evident.

John was relieved that his daughter seemed to take for granted that he and Leah would have a date after they dropped her off. He was also relieved that he didn't have to make an effort at conversation, and he thought Leah probably was, too. Eventually, though, they would be alone in the close confines of his vehicle, and he would have to try to clear the air between them, whether they had dinner at a restaurant or returned home to go their separate ways.

It was agreed that Gracie would stay until midafternoon the following day, and that Tiffany's parent's would bring her home. John and Leah exchanged hugs and kisses with the little girl, spent a few minutes talking to Tiffany's mother, then found themselves back in the Jeep, a strained silence settling between them as John pulled away from the curb.

With a sidelong glance at Leah, he saw that she'd turned her face away and was staring out the window, her fingers twisting together nervously in her lap. Mentally he cursed himself all over again for causing her such unnecessary stress. He hated that she was so uncomfortable in his presence, but he knew he had only himself to blame. And only he could make things better between them again, right here and right now.

"Hey," he said softly.

Keeping one hand on the steering wheel and his eyes on the road, he reached over and gently traced a line along the back of Leah's hand with his fingertips.

Startled, she whipped her head around and looked at him, her eyes shadowed with dismay.

"What?" she asked, drawing away from his touch.

Sighing quietly, John put his free hand back on the steering wheel. He had hoped she would make things easy for him, but he couldn't blame her for resisting even his mildest advance.

"We need to talk about what happened between us earlier in the week."

"I think we've both said all that needs saying," she replied, her tone matter-of-fact. "We got a little carried away and it was a mistake on both our parts. Rest assured I haven't gotten, nor will I ever get, any false ideas about…us. You've been lonely and I was convenient and, well, we've both agreed it won't happen again, haven't we? Personally I can't think of anything else to say about the matter.''

Frustrated at having his own callous words tossed back at him with such seeming nonchalance, John had a hard time keeping his own voice level. Much as he wanted to rage at his crude dismissal of the kisses they'd shared, he would only end up causing Leah more anguish.

''I had no right and certainly no reason to say the things I did the other night. Any ideas you might have gotten were strictly my doing. I was the one who initiated our…encounters. I was the one who kissed you in a suggestive and sexually intimate way, and I didn't do it just because you happened to be available.''

''Then why did you say those things to me, John? Why did you push me away like I was a…a poisonous toad?'' Leah demanded. The pain in her voice lanced through him with knifepoint precision.

''Because we're better off just being friends, Leah, the way we've always been.''

''You didn't kiss me as if you thought of me as just a friend or *wanted* me as just a friend. I'm not so naive that I can't recognize passion when I feel it, and you kissed me with real passion, John. Not just once, but both times we were alone together in the kitchen,'' she retorted, confused and angry all over again. ''You say you want one thing from me, then you act like you want something else. And when I respond to the way you're acting in what would normally be considered a positive way, you push me away. I don't know what you really want from me, but I do know that the things you've said to me, the things you've done, have been hurtful. And I haven't done anything, at least as far as I can see, to deserve that kind of treatment from you.''

"I'm sorry, Leah, I really am.''

"Don't be sorry, John. Just decide what it is you want from me once and for all. I know you loved Caro, and I know you miss her more than anyone can imagine, but I'm not Caro and I never will be—''

"It's not Caro I want, Leah,'' John cut in as he pulled over to the side of the road and slammed on the brakes. "But because of her...because of what happened to her...''

His voice trailed off and he stared miserably out the windshield. With a shock of recognition, he realized where he'd driven during his conversation with Leah.

"Oh, hell,'' he muttered, gripping the steering wheel in both hands.

Leah, too, suddenly realized where they were. Frowning, she looked at him.

"We're at the cemetery,'' she said, stating the obvious.

Indeed, they were—just outside the iron gates, in fact. But what on earth had prompted him to go there tonight of all nights?

John couldn't remember consciously driving in the direction of the cemetery. Nor had he had this particular destination in mind as they'd left Tiffany's house. And yet being there now seemed entirely appropriate somehow, especially considering the direction his thoughts had been taking.

"Is this where Caro is buried?'' Leah asked quietly.

"Yes, it is.''

"I've never been to her gravesite. I know I should

have come to pay my respects by now. I've been in town almost two weeks. But I couldn't seem to bring myself to make the trip here on my own.''

''I'll take you there,'' he said, unable to deny the seeming fate of the moment.

John drove through the iron gates along the narrow, blacktop road, past the small, wood-frame chapel, white with dark green shutters. The lowering sun lent the stained-glass windows a sparkle, but sent shadows looming in the groves of trees guarding the gravesites. He pulled up to the curb eventually, some distance from the entry gates, and parked near a gravel path that led to a small, plain, white-marble headstone.

Up close, it was possible to see the tiny seated angel carved into the lower right-hand corner as Georgette had requested. A tribute to the daughter she had often called her angel. Otherwise, the monument held only Caro's name and the dates of her birth and death. The flowers that John, Georgette and Cameron had left there for Mother's Day were now gone of course, but the grass grew in a thick, lush and beautiful blanket.

''I still have a hard time believing I'll never see her again,'' Leah said, her voice thick with tears. ''She was so vibrant, so alive, and then she was just…gone. Because I was out of the country when I first heard that she'd died, and because several weeks had passed since the accident and her funeral, her death never seemed quite real to me. Even coming back to Missoula, staying with you and Gracie, I've never really faced how permanent her absence is. I knew in my mind that she was never coming back, but in my heart…''

Her words trailing off, Leah swiped at the tears on her face.

Wishing there was some way he could comfort her,

as well as himself, John put an arm around her shoulders and drew her close. Knowing he was responsible for Leah's anguish just intensified his own, though, and the only thoughts he wanted to voice were bitter, angry and self-condemning.

He never should have brought Leah here, and for the life of him, he couldn't say why he had. It hadn't been a deliberate act on his part, he'd already determined that much. He hadn't even realized where he was going until he'd pulled to the curb. Nor did he have the first clue what he'd hoped to accomplish by bringing Leah to Caro's gravesite.

Maybe he had simply needed to remind himself forcefully of why a sexually intimate relationship with her was out of the question. And standing in the place where his wife was buried, he had certainly gotten the necessary wake-up call.

Before they'd reached the cemetery, he'd been much too close to revealing the depth of his feelings for Leah. His defenses had been down, and her probing questions had hit closer and closer to the mark. He'd almost admitted that it was *she* he loved, and what a mistake that would have been! Such a revelation would have meant making other revelations that would very likely have driven Leah out of his life forever. And that was a risk he wasn't about to take.

"We'd better go," he said, his voice gruff as he turned her toward the gravel path leading back to the Jeep. "They close the gates at seven o'clock most nights."

"I'm sorry, John. I didn't mean to get all weepy."

"You're certainly entitled to cry for Caro, Leah," he said, moving his arm from her shoulders and shoving his hands in the pockets of his shorts. "Believe me, I have."

"I know. I'm sorry."

"There's no need to be. I'm dealing with it. So just stop apologizing, okay?"

The bitterness and anger he'd been feeling had crept into his tone. But he didn't regret it. Not even when he saw how stung by it Leah was. He needed to put some distance between them, needed desperately to do it as a means of self-preservation. And he was willing to use whatever method was likely to work the best.

As he opened the door of the car for her, he caught a glimpse of her confused and hurt expression, but it only made him harden his heart toward her all the more. She didn't say anything, for which he was grateful. She just climbed into the passenger seat and sat with her hands folded neatly in her lap as he closed the door and went around to the driver's side.

He settled behind the steering wheel, inserted his key in the ignition, started the engine and pulled away from the curb. All the while, Leah remained still and silent beside him, her face turned to the side window. And all the while he felt like more and more of a jerk.

"Would you care to stop somewhere for dinner?" he asked after several minutes, making an effort to sound contrite.

Leah glanced at him, surprise evident in her red-rimmed eyes, then quickly looked away again.

"No, thanks. I'm not really hungry," she replied without any hint of the admonition he deserved.

John wasn't sure if he was more relieved or disappointed by her response, but he chose to accept it at face value. He wasn't very hungry, either, and he wasn't sure he was up to the effort of showing Leah the kindness and consideration she deserved when he was in such a self-contemptuous frame of mind. He would only risk turning his disgust with himself on her, and she had put up with enough of that from him already.

"Maybe another time, then."

"Yes, maybe another time," she agreed without enthusiasm.

They drove the rest of the way to the house in a strained silence. Once there, John knew he couldn't go inside with her. Even if she retreated to her room and he confined himself to his study, the temptation to seek her out with one lame excuse or another would be impossible to resist.

He would be better off going to the lab at the university and cooling his heels there for a few hours. By the time he returned home again, Leah would be fast asleep, and short of finding the house in flames, he would have no logical reason to disturb her.

She didn't seem the least bit surprised when he pulled into the driveway and left the engine running. And when he told her he was going to the lab for a while, instead of questioning him or expressing concern as she might have once done, she merely looked resigned.

"Don't work too hard," she said as she climbed out, not bothering to meet this gaze before she closed the door, then slowly made her way up the sidewalk to the front door.

They could have had an enjoyable evening together, John thought as he backed out of the driveway and headed down the street. If only he had kept his mouth shut about the kisses they'd shared and stayed away from the cemetery. He was the one who kept insisting he wanted Leah only as a friend, but then, he kept mucking it up by letting his true desire for her get the better of him.

Not for the first time, he wondered if deep down he

wanted to tell Leah the truth about the night Caro died. But what good would that do either one of them? Leah would finally see him as the contemptible man he really was. And he would gain no absolution for his sins because he simply didn't deserve any.

Some things really were better left unspoken, he told himself as he pulled into his parking place at the university—especially those things that could never be taken back once they were uttered.

There were a couple of other vehicles parked there, but otherwise the area was deserted. The building that housed his lab looked equally unoccupied, but then, it was Saturday night. Only those with no other life would be cooped up in an office or a laboratory working alone, and suddenly John didn't want to be one of them. He wanted to be with other people, wanted to eat a burger and drink a couple of beers and listen to some jukebox music, and he knew just where to go to find all those things.

Leaving his Jeep in the lot, he walked quickly across the campus quadrangle to the bridge over the Clark Fork River and the crowded, smoky bar and grill perched nearby, overlooking the water. Inside, he was greeted in short order by a rowdy group of his graduate students, and soon he found himself crowded into a booth with them near the tiny dance floor, beer in hand and burger on the way.

He could think of better ways to spend a Saturday night—with Leah, for one. But he could also think of worse ways. So he sat back and sipped his beer, determined to enjoy the company he'd chosen to keep.

Chapter Twelve

Leah prowled around the house, unable to settle down, her thoughts whirling in several different directions. She replayed in her mind the conversation she'd had with John after they'd dropped off Gracie at Tiffany's house, their unexpected arrival at the cemetery gates, the odd way his mood had shifted as they stood by Caro's grave and the strained drive back to the house.

As twilight deepened the shadows in the house, Leah's restlessness seemed to increase. She knew she should turn on some lights, pop a CD in the player and fix something to eat. She'd told John she wasn't hungry when he'd offered to take her out to dinner, and she hadn't been at the time. But now she was craving something hot and greasy and not of her own making.

She was also craving company, and that brought to mind the other friends she had in Missoula. Susan would be home with her family or out with her husband on a

Saturday night, though, and Sarah was an hour's drive away in Hamilton. Debra, however, answered the phone at her mother's house on the second ring and seemed just as eager to hang out with a friend as Leah was. They readily agreed to meet at the bar and grill overlooking the river near the university campus in the thirty minutes it would take each of them to get there.

Leah exchanged her shorts for her denim skirt, grabbed her keys, her wallet and denim jacket, and decided to walk the relatively short distance so she wouldn't have to spend time finding a parking place. She heard the music a block away and saw Debra waiting for her at the door, and knew she had made the right decision.

The place was as noisy and as smoky and as full of people as Leah remembered it being eight years ago. They found a tiny table for two in a dark corner and hailed a passing waitress to order beers and hamburgers without even bothering to check the menu. With the jukebox blaring, conversation was almost impossible, so they sat back and sipped their beers and watched the couples gyrating on the dance floor as they waited for their food to arrive.

Several people, all of whom Debra knew from her more frequent visits home, stopped by to say hello. When the tempo of the music downshifted, one young man returned and asked Debra to dance. Leah munched contentedly on her hamburger, glad to see her friend having such a good time.

As another slow song started and Debra stayed on the dance floor, Leah finished eating, then pushed her plate aside. She'd just taken a last swallow of beer when another of the men who knew Debra came up to the table and asked her to dance.

He was just about her height with neatly trimmed blond hair, a mischievous smile and polite manner, and she remembered Debra introducing him as Rick. She also remembered how much fun she'd had dancing at the dance hall in Hamilton. Standing, she put her hand in his and let him lead her to the floor.

He turned out to be a pretty good dancer, guiding her carefully among the other swaying couples, holding her close, but not so close as to make her feel uncomfortable. He made an attempt at conversation, too, asking about Chicago, about how long she planned to stay in Missoula, and if she'd been up to Glacier National Park since the Going to the Sun Road had opened for the summer season.

Leah was about to say she hadn't been up to Glacier yet but hoped to get there before the crowds of tourists grew too big when someone loomed over Rick and tapped him on the shoulder.

"I'd like to cut in, please," the man said, and Leah recognized his voice. John.

"Do you know this guy?" Rick asked, not releasing her immediately.

"Yes, he's a friend of mine," she replied, eyeing John warily.

He didn't look happy to see her, not happy at all. She wasn't especially happy to see him, either, but she didn't want to cause a scene. And that would likely happen if he didn't get his way, considering the obstinate expression that had settled across his handsome features.

"Oh, well, then…okay. Catch you later, Leah."

Rick moved out of the way graciously and John took his place, one hand clasping her waist, the other capturing her hand and holding it against his chest. He held her a little more firmly, a little more closely and a lot more possessively than Rick had, but the gleam in his eyes bordered on angry.

Deciding not to let him intimidate her, especially since she had no reason to *feel* intimidated, Leah flashed him one of her brightest smiles.

"Well, John Bennett, fancy meeting you here," she said. "I guess you finished up at the lab early, huh?"

"I didn't go to the lab," he replied in icy tones.

"I thought you said you had work to do."

"And I thought you said you weren't hungry. Looked to me like you didn't seem to have any trouble polishing off that burger you ordered," he shot back.

"Spying on me, were you?" She injected a little teasing into her tone, hoping to lighten his mood.

"I saw you come in with your friend…"

"Debra," she supplied. "She's in Missoula visiting her mother. She also went out with Susan, Sarah and me on Tuesday night."

"And you *are* extremely easy to watch," he continued with a wry smile, making an obvious attempt to relax.

"Flattery will get you nowhere," she chided him. "You were rude to Rick, cutting in on him the way you did."

"I couldn't help myself." He pulled her closer still. "And Rick seems to have survived."

With a tip of his chin, he directed her attention to the young man now dancing with a tiny redhead, and Leah couldn't help but laugh.

"Why wouldn't you have dinner with me?" John asked after a few moments.

Leah sighed quietly and rested her head on his shoulder, sure that he must know the answer to his question.

Yet he seemed to be waiting for her to make some response.

"You seemed so angry, so upset again after we left the cemetery. I thought you were just being polite when you asked if I wanted to stop for dinner. I thought that all you really wanted to do was be alone. Then you took off for the lab, only that's not where you went, after all."

"I thought I wanted to be alone when I dropped you off at the house. But when I got to the campus parking lot, I realized I didn't want to be there, either. I wanted to be with people." He feathered a light kiss on her cheek. "Hell, Leah, I wanted to be with you, but I couldn't…"

In the smoky darkness, with the music playing and other couples dancing around them, Leah looked up at him, hearing the same words he'd spoken before with the same caveat of "couldn't, shouldn't" hinted at but never completely explained. She wasn't sure if she was more confused or angry. She didn't like being played with as if she were a toy, and she certainly didn't appreciate having her emotions tugged one way, then another.

She was about to say as much when John bent his head and kissed her, long and slow and deep, as they continued to sway together to the beat of the music.

Leah didn't want to be sidetracked so easily. Knew, in fact, that she'd probably end up regretting it. But there was something irresistible about John's kiss, something that made it much too satisfying to just give in and enjoy the moment.

After a few seconds of silence, another song started playing on the jukebox. The tempo was faster and it seemed to bring him to his senses, and as quickly as he'd claimed her mouth, he pulled away again. Leah could feel the sudden tension in his body and she could sense in him the same mental rearing back that had occurred every time he'd kissed her before.

She wanted to grab him by his shirtfront and give him a good, hard shake.

She wanted to demand that he explain his erratic behavior, and she wanted his explanation to be an honest, detailed one, rather than the shaded intimations he'd offered her already.

But they were in the middle of a very public place, and she knew better than to think she'd get any answers out of him there. He was already apologizing, hand shoved through his hair, eyes on the floor. But she refused to tell him it was all right, refused to say she understood. She simply turned on her heel and walked away.

Heading for the door, Leah stopped only to tell Debra she was going home. Then she was out in the clear, cold, night air, taking deep, calming breaths and walking fast without a backward glance.

He wouldn't follow her, she was sure of that. But he would come home eventually. She planned to be waiting for him where he'd least expect her and she planned to get some answers out of him once and for all. She couldn't tolerate living the way she had been, her hopes soaring one minute, only to be dashed the next.

She had to find out what was going on in John's head. Either she was more to him than just a friend or she wasn't. And if his love for Caro remained so great that he could never really love *her,* then she had a right to know that, as well.

John's Jeep wasn't in the driveway when Leah got to the house, but she hadn't expected it to be. If he ran true to form, he would stay away until well after midnight, then creep home when he thought she'd be in her room fast asleep.

Well, tonight he was in for a big surprise.

Without lingering, Leah took a hot shower, washing the scent of cigarette smoke from her hair and body. Then she put on a pair of sweatpants and a loose-fitting T-shirt, deciding she might as well be as comfortable as possible while she waited for him.

Deceptive though she knew it was, albeit for a good cause, she closed the door of her room, crossed the kitchen and headed for the staircase. On the second floor, she hesitated only a few moments before she entered John's study. Guided by the moonlight slanting through the partially closed blinds, she made her way to the small leather sofa without tripping over anything.

Curling up in one corner, she lit the lamp on the end table. Though she'd brought a book with her to read, she doubted she'd be able to concentrate on it. But with the light on, John would be lured into the room—if for no other reason than to turn it off. And once he had entered his study, Leah had no intention of letting him leave again until he'd answered all her questions.

She hadn't planned to doze off. In fact, she could rarely sleep with a light on in the room, thus another reason to leave the lamp lit. It didn't work for her on that particular night, though. One minute she was trying to focus on the page she was attempting to read and the next she was coming to groggy wakefulness with John sitting on the edge of one of the sofa cushions, saying her name and gently shaking her by the shoulder.

"What are you doing up here?" he asked, sounding none too pleased to find her there.

He smelled of smoke and beer, his eyes were red-rimmed, and there was a hint of dark stubble on his cheeks and chin. As she sat up and swung her feet to the floor, Leah was tempted to make some lame excuse and scurry back to her room. Common sense warned that John was in no mood for a confrontation at that early hour of the morning. But he would never be in the mood for it, and the longer she put if off, the more painful it would be for her to continue living in his house.

"Waiting for you," she answered at last, offering him what she hoped was a mollifying smile.

"Has something happened?" he demanded, his annoyance now edged with concern. "Is Gracie all right? And Cameron and Georgette?"

"As far as I know they're all fine," she said.

"Then why…?"

"We need to talk, John, really *talk* to each other and clear the air between us. You say one thing, then do another, and it's getting harder and harder for me to understand your motivations."

Leah sensed his resistance immediately. He looked away from her, his gaze suddenly hooded, and he shifted on the sofa as if getting ready to stand and walk away.

"I never know what to expect from you, and I haven't a clue how to deal with your mood swings," she continued, putting a restraining hand on his arm to keep him from moving.

"There's nothing to discuss, Leah," he advised her curtly, shaking off her hand as he stood. "Or maybe I should say there's nothing I *want* to discuss with you, especially at one o'clock in the morning."

He started toward the doorway, but prepared as she was for just such a maneuver, she managed to move quickly past him and block his way.

"You say you care about me, but only as a friend, yet

you kiss me as if you care about me in other, more intimate ways. Then you say you *can't* want me sexually. You talk about Caro, you make vague references to the night she died, and you blame yourself. Why, John? What happened that night? Just tell me, please, so I can understand.''

He glared at her for long moments, his obvious anger at having her block his path barely contained. He stood with his fists clenched, his body rigid, his breathing hard.

Leah fully expected him to take her by the shoulders and forcibly move her out of his way. Instead, though, he spun away from her and moved to stand by his desk. He leaned against it, his back to her, his hands gripping the edge. Slowly, like a balloon losing air, he seemed to deflate. And when he spoke again, his voice was so cold, so detached and so distant that it cut through Leah like an icy wind, making her wonder if she'd made a mistake she would end up regretting.

''You want to know what happened the night Caro died?'' He straightened up again and faced her, then gestured to the sofa, his expression as bleak and uncompromising as his tone. ''Okay, have a seat and I'll tell you all about it, every gory detail.''

Her sense of trepidation increasing with each passing moment, Leah suddenly wasn't sure she wanted to finish what she'd started, after all. But if she scampered away like a frightened rabbit now, she would never be able to look John—or herself—in the eye again.

Obediently she walked over to the sofa and sat down, hands clasped in her lap, sweaty palm to sweaty palm. She drew a deep breath that did little to steady her, then looked up at him, waiting to hear what he had to say.

Chapter Thirteen

One hip propped against the edge of his desk, his arms folded protectively across his chest, John stared at the patterned blue-and-burgundy-red Persian rug on the polished wood floor of his study, trying to gather his thoughts. In the light of day he would more than likely regret what he was about to tell Leah. But at that moment the burden of maintaining his silence had become greater than he could bear.

He had only himself to blame for her questions. He was the one who'd initiated the game of advance-and-retreat with her, though he'd never intended it to be a game. He wasn't intentionally cruel by nature. But obviously and rightfully, it had begun to seem so to Leah. He owed her the answers she now demanded of him. They would be small payment for the grief he'd caused her since she'd returned to Missoula.

Once she knew the truth about him and what he'd

done to Caro, however, any romantic fantasies she'd had about him would surely disappear. Then she would be more than happy to keep him at a distance for the remainder of her stay. And at a distance, he couldn't hurt her any more than he already had.

"I know you believe that Caro and I had a wonderful marriage, close and loving and as near to perfect as any relationship between a man and a woman could be," he began, risking a glance at Leah.

She met his gaze, a small frown furrowing her forehead, but to his relief she didn't say anything. She simply waited patiently for him to continue with whatever he had to tell her.

"It wasn't anything like that, though," he went on, looking away again, his thoughts focused on the past. "Granted, we were infatuated with each other when we first met. She was so lovely, so charming and sophisticated, and she was so obviously interested in me, of all people. I admit it went to my head, being so desirable to someone like her. I remember wondering what she could possibly see in me, but not enough to really question her motives or look beyond those early days we spent together to what a long-term relationship together might be like for each of us.

"Later, much later, after Gracie was born, I realized that with Georgette's marriage to your father, Caro had been feeling abandoned all over again. First she'd lost her father when he died, then her mother when she remarried so quickly. She was also at a point in her life where she was going to be expected to start supporting herself, and she didn't really want that responsibility. Caro saw her mother happily married to a man who was going to look after her for the rest of her life, and she wanted—needed—the same thing for herself. I happened to be not only available, but also ready, willing and able to fulfill her every want and need.''

"But you loved each other, I know you did," Leah protested, her voice strained. "I was the one who introduced you. You looked at each other and I could almost feel the sparks fly between you. I saw you together all those months before your wedding, too."

"Yes, sparks flew, and we did love each other, but in a very tenuous way. We were together for several months—but only months, not even a full year—before we married. We didn't know much at all about each other, and I don't think either one of us was interested in looking beneath the surface then. If we had, we would have discovered how little we had in common."

"You don't have to have a lot in common with someone to care about her," Leah said pragmatically. "And I know that you and Caro cared about each other deeply, and about Gracie, too."

"Of course we cared about each other and about Gracie, but we began drifting apart even before she was born. Looking back, I sometimes think Caro might have been on the verge of ending our marriage before she found out she was pregnant. It wasn't something we'd planned...."

John paused as he remembered the words Caro had hurled at him the night she died. But he wasn't ready to give Leah that bit of information just yet.

"Caro seemed happy enough, though," he went on. "And I thought having a baby would help close some of the distance between us. For a while it did, but then...we started going our separate ways more and more. And when we were together, it seemed like all we did was argue."

"Couples argue all the time—" Leah began.

"I know that," John cut in angrily. "But eventually they kiss and make up, just like you told Gracie. Only we didn't, because neither of us really wanted to. Caro started throwing out the occasional comment about leaving me, but I didn't take her seriously. I didn't want to take her seriously. We had Gracie to consider, and as far as I was concerned, having a child made splitting up out of the question.

"I didn't want my daughter to live through the same horror I did when my parents divorced. And because I was so damned stubborn, so damned bullheaded, I robbed my daughter of the mother she needed and loved."

He paused again and scrubbed a hand over his face, trying to calm the anger he felt toward himself, afraid Leah would think it was directed at her.

"John, you didn't," she insisted as she stood and started to move in his direction. "Caro died in an accident—"

He put up a hand to ward her off, glaring at her in the same cold and dispassionate manner in which he spoke.

"Caro would never have been out on the road with Gracie that night if I'd only agreed to what she wanted. She came to me after she'd put Gracie to bed and told me she'd decided to file for divorce. I said there was no way I would ever willingly agree to give her a divorce, and if she pushed me into it, I'd make sure I got sole custody of our daughter. She tried to reason with me, but I wouldn't listen to a word she said. Finally I told her if she was so determined to leave me, she could go any time she wanted, but she wasn't taking Gracie with her. She stormed upstairs, I assumed to pack a bag. But when she came down again only a few minutes later, she was holding Gracie in her arms and had only her purse and car keys in her hand.''

Unable to continue, John swallowed hard, but as Leah started toward him again, he warned her off with another wave of his hand.

"No, let me finish," he said, his voice harsh. "I went after her as she headed for the door. There was no way I was going to let her take Gracie with her. I was shouting at her, demanding she give me my daughter. She turned to look at me and something in her eyes stopped me cold. Then she said, almost conversationally, that...that Gracie wasn't my daughter, and she could...she could take her anywhere she wanted and I wouldn't be able to stop her."

The pain lancing through him as he repeated Caro's words to him that fateful night literally took his breath away. Again he paused in his recitation and swallowed, then forced himself to finish what he'd started.

"I just stood there staring at her, trying to understand what she was saying, trying to comprehend something that was totally, completely inconceivable to me. And in those few moments, Caro walked out the door in the middle of a rainstorm.

"I should have gone after her. I should have tried to keep her from getting in her car, but for the longest time I just stood in the entryway, frozen in place. Eventually I came up here to my study and sat in the dark. I assumed Caro had taken Gracie to your father's house. I thought I'd find them both there in the morning and would try to sort things out then. But the telephone rang and it was someone calling from the hospital, and...well, you know the rest." Blinking at the sting of tears in his eyes, John avoided Leah's gaze as he concluded quietly, "Caro is dead because of me, Leah, because of *me*. And not only was Gracie badly hurt, now she's also going to grow up without the one real parent she had.''

"John, no, none of that is true, none of it," Leah insisted.

Standing beside him, she reached out and touched his chin with gentle fingertips, turning his face so that he was forced to look at her despite his initial resistance.

"You didn't force Caro to go out into a storm. She left here with Gracie of her own free will, more than likely just to show you that she could. We both know what a volatile temper she could have, especially when she wanted something done her way and couldn't get it without pitching a fit. She used bad judgment to prove a point, and she had an accident that cost her her life and injured Gracie. Yes, you argued with her, but that was only one of the factors involved, and a very minor one at that, all things considered.''

John met Leah's gaze, wanting to believe that what she said was true, but he'd spent a year already convinced of his own culpability, and it was almost impossible for him to think otherwise. There was still the matter of Gracie's parentage to consider, too.

Seeming to read his mind, Leah added quietly, "I don't know what possessed Caro to say what she did about Gracie, but I, for one, don't believe it's true. She never once indicated to me that she'd ever had an affair or that anyone but you had fathered your daughter. We got to be really good friends over the years, John. We were very close and we shared a lot. I think she would have told me if she'd been with someone else.

"There's the physical resemblance between you and Gracie to consider, too. It's subtle, but it's most definitely there. Maybe you haven't noticed, but the color of her eyes is exactly like yours, and so is her expression when she's in a thoughtful mood. Of course, there are tests you can have done to determine whether or not she's your daughter if you're still not convinced. Though I think she is in every way that really matters, don't you?''

''I'm not sure what I think anymore,'' he admitted, taking her hand in his and clinging to it like a drowning man would a lifeline.

He had been convinced that Leah would turn away from him in disappointment and disgust once she knew what had happened the night Caro died. Instead, she had considered the circumstances with amazing rationality. She was right about Caro's temper. His wife had never liked being thwarted, and up until that fateful night, he had almost always acquiesced to her wishes.

But he had felt so strongly about keeping their family together for Gracie's sake that he hadn't been willing to give in that one time. And Caro had chosen to punish him for it in the cruelest way she could think of. She had endangered herself and their daughter—yes, *their* daughter—because, for once in his life, he had dared to stand up to her.

''You've been beating yourself up for something that wasn't your fault,'' Leah chided him gently, holding tightly to his hand. ''All you meant to do was try to save your marriage and hold your family together. You couldn't have known that Caro would say or do what she did. And her death was the result of an accident, one she never would have had if she hadn't chosen to drive so fast on a rain-slick road.''

For the first time in the year since his wife's death, John experienced a heretofore unimaginable lightening of his spirits. Leah's softly spoken words were a balm to his bruised and beleaguered soul. The bitterness and anger, the guilt and the anguish that had been his constant companions loosened their grip on him, releasing him into a new and startling world where long-lost hopes and dreams could finally be fulfilled. And at the center of that world, at the center of those hopes and dreams, stood his lovely, loving Leah.

Wordlessly, he pushed away from the desk and put his arms around her. Wordlessly, he held her close and rubbed his cheek against her silky hair, unable to stem the flow of tears that finally trickled from his eyes.

"It's all right, John," she murmured, her voice thick with her own tears. "Everything is going to be all right now."

"Thanks to you, Leah. Only thanks to you."

"All I did was listen, and that's all you really needed. You loved Caro and because of that, you did your best to hold your marriage together. You were a wonderful husband and you are a wonderful father. So stop beating yourself up, okay?"

"Okay," he agreed.

Her teasing tone—an obvious effort to lighten his mood—made him smile as he looked down at her.

She met his gaze steadily and smiled back, and his heart squeezed with a sudden, almost visceral longing. There were no secrets between them anymore, and no lingering fear on his part that he was unworthy of her love. She now knew the truth about him and Caro, and she thought no less of him. Maybe now, finally, he could begin to show her, to tell her, how much he wanted to right all the wrong turns he'd taken with her in the past.

"Leah, my lovely Leah," he muttered, then bent his head and claimed her mouth with a fierce, possessive kiss that still only hinted at the depth of his long-denied desire.

Leah clung to John, welcoming his kiss and responding to it with a fervor of her own. Understanding at last the true depth of the emotional agony he'd suffered as a result of Caro's death, she couldn't stop herself from offering the comfort he so desperately seemed to need. Finally released from the torment of the false beliefs about himself he had harbored over the past year, he had to be experiencing an enormous sense of relief. And in the sudden unexpected respite he was now turning to her, his most trusted friend.

She didn't allow herself to be fooled into believing that his feelings for her compared in any way to the feelings he'd once had for Caro—probably *still* had for her. He'd never actually said that he had stopped loving his wife, that *he* had wanted to be free of *her*.

Divorcing had been Caro's idea, and though John had said he opposed it for Gracie's sake, Leah couldn't help but believe he hadn't wanted to break his emotional bond with her, either. They might have drifted apart, as he had said, but Leah had seen with her own eyes how much he'd loved Caro eight years ago. That kind of love never really faded away. It lingered in one's heart and mind for all eternity.

For now, though, for these special moments out of time, she wouldn't think any more about Caro and what she'd meant—what she would always mean—to John. For now, Leah wanted only to take what she could have of him and be happy. It might not be all she'd once hoped it would be. But she'd wanted for so long to be held by him, to be kissed by him, to be desired by him in the most intimate way, that even knowing he would never love her as he'd loved Caro, she couldn't push him away.

Better to accept what he *could* offer her and have

wonderful memories to hold close to her heart than to go on aching with emptiness as she had for so many years already.

"Leah?" John raised his head a fraction, breaking their kiss, his voice soft and questioning, his pale gray eyes searching hers as if seeking permission. "I want you so much...I need you so much...."

"I need you, too, John," she whispered in reply, tracing the hard line of his jaw with her fingertips.

"Let me make love to you...please?"

The tenderness in his voice made it impossible for her to speak. She could only nod her head in solemn, heartfelt agreement. He acknowledged her acquiescence wordlessly, as well, his gentle smile speaking volumes as he took her by the hand and led her out of the study.

In the hallway he paused, then moved toward his bedroom, but Leah tugged on his hand, turning him toward the staircase, instead. When he eyed her with a puzzled look on his face, she shrugged and smiled slightly.

"I'd feel more comfortable if we went to my room," she explained.

It was probably foolish of her—she was in Caro's house, after all. But she didn't want to feel her stepsister's presence any more than absolutely necessary. And in the bedroom Caro had shared with John, her presence, even after a year, would surely still be strong.

"I'm sorry. I wasn't thinking," John said apologetically, seeming to understand. And then, as they reached the bottom of the staircase, he paused again abruptly. "Birth control," he muttered, eyeing her with sudden dismay. "Talk about not thinking—I don't have anything to protect you."

"I do," she assured him, then laughed at the suddenly assessing look he gave her. "No, I don't carry condoms with me everywhere I go with the hope of getting lucky. Your former nanny, in her haste to get away, just happened to leave behind an unopened box.''

"Hey, I never thought you did," John protested, pulling her into his arms. ''But I wouldn't have minded tonight, especially if my former nanny hadn't come through for us. Apparently she was good for something, after all.''

Allowing Leah no chance for further comment, he kissed her soundly on the mouth, then scooped her up into his arms and carried her the rest of the way to her room. With one hand, he pulled back the quilt and cotton blanket, then set her gently on the bed. In the darkness he loomed over her, tall, muscular and incredibly masculine, desire radiating from him. Her senses heightened to an unbearable level, Leah felt her heartbeat quicken in anticipation.

"Where are they?" he asked.

"In the medicine cabinet," she answered, a tremor in her voice as she leaned back against the pillows.

"Give me five minutes."

As he turned away from her, Leah pulled her T-shirt over her head. Shimmying out of her sweatpants and slipping under the covers, she heard the shower go on. A few minutes later, as good as his word, John reappeared, his damp hair slicked back. He was naked, as she'd never seen him, and he held the box of condoms in his hand.

She stared at him, unable to help herself. Noting the ready evidence of his desire for her, her breath caught in her throat. For several moments she couldn't seem to move, and when she met his gaze, he offered her a gentle smile.

"Let me love you, Leah," he said.

"Yes, please..."

Slowly she turned back the covers, making a place for him.

He lay down beside her and held out his arms. With a soft sigh, she went to him willingly, savoring the warmth of his skin against hers, the hard, demanding press of his masculinity against the nest of her femininity. For long moments he simply held her securely in his arms, one hand cupping her hip, the other ever so gently stroking her hair.

Though her heart still beat a rapid tattoo, she gradually began to relax. Breathing in the clean, soapy, yet distinctively masculine scent of him, she explored the muscular contours of his shoulders, his back and his incredibly firm buttocks. Tangling his fingers in her hair possessively, John tipped her head back and feathered light kisses over all her face, gracing her forehead, her cheeks, her chin, the tip of her nose, her eyelids and earlobes with tiny nibbles enhanced by the roughness of his beard.

As he worked his way down along the curve of her neck to her shoulders, the crest of one breast, then the other, his mouth became more demanding, sucking, biting and licking, teasing her senses with the promise of pleasure unlike any she'd ever known. The hand he'd placed on her hip moved to the inside of her thighs, stroking with first the merest whisper of a touch, then with a deeper delving that made her shift and strain for more.

"Not yet," he growled, looking up at her, the passionate light in his eyes searing into her soul.

Leah wanted to beg him for the physical release her body craved. Yet at the same time she never wanted the exquisite sensuality she was experiencing in his arms to end. Hands braced on his shoulders, she whimpered as he played with her nipples, tugging on first one, then the other with his teeth, then laving them with his warm, wet, velvety tongue. When he cupped her womanhood in his hand, holding her firmly at the place where she was most sensitive, the combined sensations had her digging her heels into the mattress and arching her body with a wantonness she'd never imagined she possessed.

Easing away from her, John sheathed himself in a condom, then spread her legs wide and braced himself over her on his forearms. Again he threaded one hand through her hair, his gaze holding hers. Sliding his other arm under hips, he lifted her into his first, tentative thrust.

"Okay?" he asked, his voice trembling with the effort he made to hold back until he was sure she was with him.

"Oh, yes...yes...."

She reached up, cupped his face in her hands and pulled his head down to kiss him as he thrust again, this time without reserve. Burying his manhood in her to the hilt, he claimed her with a primal, triumphal growl.

Leah met him thrust for thrust, hovering just on the edge of fulfillment, seeking but not quite finding the ultimate pleasure she knew must come. Then John reached between their heaving bodies, stroking her with a clever, knowing fingertip, and her world exploded into a shimmering rapture that had her crying out his name. Clinging to him fiercely, she felt the tremors racking her body blend with his as he, too, found release.

After a while John eased his weight off her, rolling to his side as their breathing began to slow to a more normal rate. But he still held her close, as if as unwilling as she to break the deeply intimate connection Leah thought, gladly cuddling close. He pulled up the covers

to ward off the chill breeze drifting through the open
windows.

But for the longest time he didn't speak, and neither
did she. She didn't want to disturb the spell his lovemaking had cast over her. And she didn't want to disturb
the contentment she'd found, if only temporarily, in his
arms.

Finally, however, John mumbled an apology, let go
of her to slip out of bed and headed for the bathroom.
Leah sighed quietly and reached out to smooth her hand
over the warm place beside her he'd left behind. She
was surprised when he came back, climbed into her bed
again and gathered her into his arms.

She wasn't sure what she'd expected. Probably that
he would make some excuse and go upstairs to his own
room. But he seemed perfectly happy, not to mention
perfectly at ease, staying right there with her. And she
certainly wasn't going to put up any protest. She was
going to snuggle as close to him as she could and savor
the peacefulness being with him in such a way brought
to her heart and soul.

John held her quietly for a while, his arms around her
forming a loose yet protective circle as she rested her
head against his chest. His breathing was so deep and
even that she thought he must have fallen asleep. But
then he spoke, his breath warm against her forehead, his
voice edged with the faintest hint of uncertainty.

"I don't know what to say, Leah," he began. "I don't
know how to begin to tell you—"

"Shush," she said as she pressed her fingertips to his
lips and leaned back far enough to look at him. "You
don't need to say anything. I understand, John."

He seemed relieved to hear her words, and that, in
turn, eased Leah's anxiety. She wasn't ready yet to hear

him reiterate his earlier warning to her. She knew all too well already that he didn't want her getting any false ideas, and she wasn't. For now, though, she wanted at least to pretend a little longer that he'd come to her for more than just the comfort she'd so willingly, and so delightedly, offered him.

John rubbed his cheek against her hair and tightened his hold on her almost imperceptibly, then yawned hugely, making Leah laugh.

"Tired?" she asked.

"Just a little. How about you?"

"Just a little, too."

"Sleep, then. I'll be here when you wake up."

"You will?"

"Oh, yes, I most certainly will. I promise not to wake you up too early, though."

"So you're going to wake me up, huh? I thought maybe you'd let me sleep late since it's—" Leah glanced at the clock on the nightstand "—almost two-thirty in the morning."

"I said not too early. But I want some time with you when I can have you all to myself before Gracie's home again," he said, nibbling suggestively at her earlobe.

"And why would you want me all to yourself?" she asked with a tiny, satisfied smile.

"If you weren't so tired, I could show you right now."

"I said I was only a little tired. You're the one who yawned, and very rudely, I might add."

"Suddenly I'm not feeling the least bit sleepy."

"Suddenly neither am I. Do you want to raid the refrigerator for a midnight snack?"

"It's way past midnight, and I've got a much better

idea,'' he growled as he eased slowly down her body, his eyes gleaming mischievously in the dark.

''And what would that be?''

''I'd rather show than tell.'' He pressed a wet, open-mouthed kiss against her belly. ''Unless you have any objections.''

''Oh, no, none at all,'' Leah breathed as he moved lower still and put his mouth on her again.

Chapter Fourteen

To his amazement, John slept more deeply and more peacefully than he had in years, cradling Leah protectively close in his arms after making love to her a second time. Though why, upon waking with her warm, pliant body nestled next to his, he should be so surprised he didn't know.

He had bared his soul to her in the wee hours of the morning. He had shared with her the truth not only about his relationship with Caro in recent years, but also about his perceived role in her tragic death. And Leah, his loving Leah, hadn't thought any less of him.

She had viewed the past from a different, much less personal perspective than he could have ever done on his own. And she had quietly, yet unbendingly pointed out the flaws in his own self-abasing scrutiny of the events he had never really been able to control.

He'd had a right to want to hold his marriage together

for Gracie's sake, as much right as Caro had had to want to end it, whatever her reasons. And it had been Caro, not he, who had chosen to go out in a raging storm in a careless state of anger, taking their daughter with her.

Would Caro still be alive if he hadn't argued with her that fateful night?

More than likely, but then, she would also more than likely be alive if *she* hadn't driven off late at night in the middle of a storm.

Lying there with Leah, her slow, even breathing a sure sign that she still slept soundly, John silently vowed to forgive himself once and for all, and to forgive Caro, as well. For he realized, finally, that at least a part of the anger, bitterness and pain he'd suffered the past year had been directed at her. He had thought for a long time that he blamed only himself for her loss, but in fact, he blamed her, too, for the thoughtless, unwarranted and explosive behavior she'd exhibited the last night of her life.

There was no going back, no changing what had happened between him and Caro. But at last he felt free to go forward with his life and to pursue the happiness he could now honestly say he deserved to have. And at the very center of the happiness he wanted not only for himself, but for Gracie, as well, was Leah.

She was everything bright and beautiful, everything kind and gracious and truly loving they could ever hope to have in their lives. Her warmth of heart was matched in full by her generosity of spirit. Last night he'd had his first taste of what a future with her could be like. Added to the glimpses he'd had of the kind of family they could be—he, Leah and Gracie—he knew that the days to come promised to be filled with more joy and contentment than he would ever have believed possible only a few days ago.

Though it had been well past three in the morning when he and Leah had finally fallen asleep and it was now just past seven, John couldn't quell the energizing exhilaration zinging along his nerve endings. He wanted to leap from the bed and drag Leah with him, laughing and likely protesting, into the shower, then tumble her back into bed for another session of exquisite lovemaking. But her pale face and the dark shadows lingering under her eyes warned him that what she needed right now more than anything else was a good, long rest.

They would have time to explore each other's wants and needs in greater depth, more than enough time, in the weeks, months and years ahead. Now that he was finally free in every way to be with Leah, John knew he could be patient. Though not too patient, he amended, aware of how his body stirred as he did nothing but look at her sleeping so tranquilly there beside him.

They had a lot of lost time to make up for, not to mention a new life together to begin planning. Leah had shown him how much she loved him last night, as *he* had shown *her*. He had tried to tell her, too, but she had obviously known it already, shushing him before he could say the words aloud. She had said that she understood, and that had been all he needed to hear to seal his future with hers.

John tried to ease away from Leah without disturbing her, but she seemed to sense his intent. She murmured softly and reached for him, her eyelids fluttering open. He could see that she wasn't really awake, however, and he didn't want to rouse her any more than he already had.

"Go back to sleep for a while. It's still early," he said

to her, keeping his voice low and his tone mellow. "I'll be close by if you need me for anything."

"Okay," she answered, sounding muzzy. She blinked a couple of times, then closed her eyes again and snuggled her face into her pillow with a slight, but wholly contented smile. "But don't let me sleep too late...."

"I won't," he assured her, smoothing a hand over her tangled hair. "I want a little more time with you all to myself before Gracie comes home."

"Said that last night," she reminded him.

"Saying it again. Hope it's okay with you."

"Definitely okay with me...."

John tucked the bedcovers up around her shoulders, gathered his clothes from the floor and reluctantly left her, once again sleeping soundly. He closed the door to her room as he went out so he wouldn't disturb her any further, at least for the time being, and padded slowly across the den.

In the kitchen, he set up the coffeemaker to brew a fresh pot, then headed upstairs to shower and put on fresh shorts and a T-shirt. After he'd dressed, he sat on the edge of the bed he'd shared with Caro and took a good look around the room.

He hadn't changed anything about the master bedroom in the past year, and so it had remained indelibly stamped with her presence. Not because he had wanted it that way, he admitted now, but because he had wanted to punish himself in every way possible. Surrounding himself with constant reminders of Caro had been equal to surrounding himself with constant reminders of his responsibility for her death.

No more, though, he acknowledged, surveying the spill of her jewelry in the box on the dresser, the clutter of bottles and pots—perfume and makeup—on the little vanity table, the clothes still hanging in the closet visible through the open door. With Gracie away and Leah sleeping, now was the time to pack away all the mementos of the past, along with the memories they embodied, and make room for all that the future seemed to promise.

Moving quietly down the stairs to the basement, John felt his spirit lightening even more. He collected several cardboard boxes, stopped in the kitchen to fill his mug with coffee, then returned to the bedroom and set to work. Slowly and methodically he sorted those things he wanted to put away for Gracie into one box, those things he thought Georgette might like to have in another, and those things to be given away to a local shelter for abused and homeless women in yet another.

He couldn't say that he didn't suffer a pang of remorse for Caro's untimely passing. She'd deserved to live a long, happy, interesting and exciting life, and he would always be sad that she wouldn't have the opportunity to do so. But he wasn't blaming himself any longer, and he wasn't blaming her. He had finally accepted the hand fate had dealt them, and he was determined to make the most of whatever time he had left himself.

By ten o'clock John had all of Caro's things packed away and the boxes labeled and stored, for the time being, in the basement. The bedroom looked entirely different, even with the same furniture and the same bed linens. He hoped that Leah would eventually feel comfortable enough in their relationship not only to share the room with him, but also to decorate it to her liking.

For now, though, he wouldn't make any more changes himself except to dust and polish the furniture and put clean sheets on the bed. It was good just to feel at peace there again, as he finally did.

Back in the kitchen he brewed a second pot of coffee, having finished off the first one on his own already. Then, hearing the sound of water running in Leah's bathroom, he scrambled eggs, toasted bread, poured orange juice into a couple of glasses and the coffee into a carafe. He found a wicker tray in the pantry and set it with the breakfast he'd prepared. Smiling to himself, he carried it to Leah's room.

She opened the door for him when he knocked and greeted him with a shy but obviously delighted smile when she saw what he had done. His smile widened with his own brand of gratification when he saw that she wore only a T-shirt and panties, and seemed in no hurry to finish dressing, despite his presence in her room.

They sat cross-legged among the tumble of sheets and blankets, pillows and quilt on her bed, the tray balanced between them, and feasted on the eggs and toast, juice and coffee.

"You were an early bird this morning, especially considering…" Leah began, then allowed her thoughts to trail off, unspoken, as she looked into the steam rising from her mug of coffee, a blush staining her cheeks a pretty shade of pink.

John couldn't help but grin with remembered satisfaction.

"I slept for a while, but when I woke up I felt too good to laze around in bed all day."

"Like me?" she asked with a mischievous twinkle in her eye.

"You were exhausted and understandably so." His grin widened even more as her blush deepened.

"Well, yes," she admitted, risking a glance at him. "Anyway, thanks for letting me sleep. I really did need it. But what have you been doing all morning? You've been so quiet."

He hesitated for a few moments, then decided that honesty was always the best policy with Leah.

"I packed away all of Caro's things. I should have done it a long time ago, but I couldn't bring myself to face it until today. Suddenly it felt like the right thing to do, though, and I'm glad now that it's finally done."

"Oh, John, you didn't do it just because…" Leah began, a look of concern shadowing her lovely face.

"I did it because I was finally ready to put the past behind me and think about the future," he said.

Seeing that they'd both finished eating, he stood and moved the tray out of the way, setting it on the dresser. Then he sat across from her on the bed again.

"But Caro was such an important part of your life for such a long time," Leah said, a searching look in her eyes as she met his gaze.

"I'm not denying that. She will always be a part of my past, *our* past really, because we both cared about her. We'll certainly never forget her. I don't think she would want either one of us to allow our memories of her to be a cause for continued unhappiness, though. She had her selfish moments—we all do. But she was never truly mean-spirited, except maybe when she said I wasn't Gracie's father, and then I think she was just so desperate to get her way the night she died that she said the one thing she knew would stop me in my tracks, at least temporarily.

"The result was more tragic than she obviously anticipated, but it was a result of her doing, something I can finally admit and accept, thanks to your wise counsel. I don't think she would begrudge us our chance at happiness just because we're still alive and she isn't. Do you?''

"No, I don't think so, either," Leah said. "Caro always enjoyed life and she always wanted everyone around her to enjoy life too much for that to be possible. That's why I miss her so much and why I know you miss her, too."

Though Leah smiled as she spoke, she still seemed unable to let go of the sadness and regret she was so obviously feeling. John wondered if he had been wise to bring Caro into their conversation at all that morning. He didn't want his disastrous past with Caro to overshadow the promise of the future he now saw with Leah. As he had said, Caro would always be with them, but hopefully no longer in a way that would cause either of them to suffer any more remorse than they already had.

"Hey, what's done is done." Reaching out, he brushed her hair away from her face, then put his hand on the back of her neck and drew her close for a gentle, reassuring kiss.

Leah scooted across the bed and into John's arms willingly, opening her mouth to his teasing tongue, allowing him to claim her with the same possessiveness as he had the night before. It was easier not to think when he pulled her into his lap, put his mouth on hers and slipped his hands under her T-shirt to caress her breasts.

She couldn't analyze too closely the fact that John had kept his bedroom as a virtual shrine to Caro until today. Nor could she consider as completely as she probably should that he would always choose to excuse even the most hurtful things Caro had said and done to him.

All Leah was capable of doing when John made love to her was give herself up to his tender ministrations as mindlessly as she now did. Her desire for him was so great and her time with him so limited that she couldn't have denied him anything even if she had wanted to. And all she wanted was to love him in every way possible for the few weeks they had left together.

With a throaty growl, John tumbled her onto her back and quickly stripped her of the T-shirt and panties she'd put on after her shower. His need for her and the physical release she offered for a third time in less than twelve hours surprised and delighted her. She'd thought that once the initial edge had been taken off his long-celibate state, he would revert to wanting only a more cerebral relationship with her again. But he seemed as insatiable that morning as he had seemed during the night, perhaps even more so. And her need, too, was heightened to a fever pitch.

As he looked at her for the first time in the daylight, his gaze as hot and hungry as his hands roving over her, she tugged at his T-shirt, then fumbled unsuccessfully with the snap on his shorts. Taking pity on her, he shrugged out of his clothes, then stretched out beside her.

"Like what you see?" he asked, his sexy voice turning her insides to mush.

"Oh, yes," she admitted, smiling back at him, anything but demure. "And you?"

"Oh, yes, definitely."

He rolled toward her, but feeling bold, Leah pushed him onto his back again. Straddling him, she took one of the condoms from the box on the nightstand and tore open the foil wrapper.

"Taking control, are you?"

There was still a teasing note in John's voice, but underlying it Leah heard a distinctive thrill of excitement.

"Do you mind?" she asked as she slowly sheathed him with the condom, her touch as temptingly light as she could make it in an effort to enhance his pleasure to the fullest.

"Not at all."

He put his hands on her hips, lifted her and settled her on top of him again, burying himself to the hilt in the hot, wet folds of her womanhood with one well-targeted thrust.

Hands braced on John's chest, Leah leaned forward, savoring the wondrous sensation of having him deep inside her, filling her with the evidence of his desire, and trailed tiny kisses along the line of his jaw. Moving his hands from her hips, he toyed with her nipples, pressing a knowing thumb just so, then tugging with clever fingertips and sending tremors through her that soon had her writhing against him.

Cupping her face in his hands, John pulled her head down and claimed her mouth in another of his passionately all-consuming kisses as he rolled her onto her back.

"My turn now," he muttered, drawing back and plunging deeply again, then again.

Leah moved with him, arching into his steady thrusts, panting and straining, her gaze locked with his, until she couldn't hold back any longer. Calling his name, she clung to him and welcomed the mind-spinning pleasure he offered her.

Lying in his arms afterward, her breathing gradually beginning to slow, Leah tried to imprint on her memory the warmth and closeness she shared with John that sunny Sunday morning. She never wanted to forget this time they'd had together. She never *would* forget, she was sure.

Being with him in such an intimately inclusive way

was an experience she had never honestly believed she'd have. Even now she had a hard time accepting the reality of it. Only the feathering of his breath against her hair and the steady beat of his heart against her cheek kept her grounded in the perfection of the present moment.

The days would pass, though, and within a few weeks she would have to face the real world again, or at least the real world as she'd always known it. John would finally have set aside the last of his pain. He would be healed again and ready to go on with his life. She would have served her purpose, helping him through a difficult passage, and it would be time for her to move off to the sidelines once more.

Eventually he would meet someone with whom to share his life. Or perhaps he'd already met her, but hadn't realized it yet, Leah amended, thinking of Dana Berry. In any case, he would be ready to make a new start, and she would be happy for him, just as she'd been happy for him when he'd married Caro eight long years ago.

"Hey, why so pensive?" he asked, giving her a hug. "What are you thinking about?"

"That if we don't get up and get dressed very soon, we're going to be awfully embarrassed when Tiffany's parents drop Gracie off," she replied, forcing herself to smile up at him in a devilish manner.

"Are you sure that's all you've got on your mind?" he prodded, his gaze still serious and his voice edged with concern. "You're not feeling…sad for any reason, are you? Because—"

"Oh, no, I'm not sad at all," she interjected hastily, afraid he might be about to remind her of those false ideas she had promised not to get, and hadn't, she added to herself before continuing. "In fact, I'm quite happy,

thank you very much. And relaxed, so very relaxed.''
She yawned and stretched and sighed in an added effort
to assure him of her overall contentment. ''Although I'll
probably need a nap later in the afternoon.''

''Maybe we could see if Tiffany would like to have
Gracie stay until after dinner. Then we could both take
a nap together,'' John suggested.

''I think it's a little late for that,'' Leah replied as the
doorbell rang. ''I'm pretty sure that's them now.''

''Oh, hell.'' Rolling off the bed, John grabbed his
shorts and T-shirt, then struggled into them as Leah
watched. ''Aren't you getting dressed, too?''

''I'll have time while you answer the door.''

''Yeah, right.'' He smiled at her as he zipped up his
shorts, then hesitated a moment more. ''Leah, you do
know…'' he began, suddenly serious again.

''Don't worry, John, I do know. Now answer the door
before they start to wonder where we are.''

As he left her bedroom, Leah gathered her own
clothes. Once again she'd managed to stave off further
discussion about her real place in John's life. Because
she did know what she was to him, what she could be
and what she could never be.

She knew why he'd turned to her for sex after his
revelations concerning the night Caro died. And she
knew that once he'd regained some of his lost self-
esteem, once he felt whole again, he wouldn't need or
want her in quite so intimate a way.

In the meantime, however, she would enjoy what time
they had together because she loved him, had always
loved him and would always love him, even when all
he expected of her was friendship.

Caro would always be his first love, his most beloved
one. That was more evident now than ever to Leah. She

might not want to think about those things of Caro's he had kept close at hand for almost a year or the firm belief he had in Caro's generous spirit. But she couldn't ignore those facts forever. And she couldn't stand in Caro's shadow as she would once John had time to make certain comparisons.

For now, she was exactly what he needed to revitalize his spirit. But only for now, not for always, and Leah had long ago decided she would rather be alone than be second-best the rest of her life.

Chapter Fifteen

Pulling into the driveway after taking Gracie to what would likely be her last visit to Dr. Berry, John saw that Leah's car wasn't in the driveway.

"It looks like Aunt Leah is still visiting her friend Sarah, in Hamilton," his daughter said, voicing the same thought he'd had with a disappointment that matched his own.

"She said she'd probably be gone until late afternoon and it's only one-thirty now," John reminded her.

"I wish she could have gone to see Dr. Berry with us, and she missed a really good lunch at the deli, too."

"I wish she could have been with us, too, Gracie. But Leah needs some time off occasionally. We tend to keep her pretty busy most days."

"She likes being with us, Daddy. I know she does 'cause she says so all the time."

"I know, sweetie."

In fact, during the three weeks that had passed since the night he had told Leah about Caro's death—the night they had also made love for the first time—he, Leah and Gracie had become more and more of a family unit, sharing a new closeness that John had never expected to experience with anyone again in his life. And yet—

"Is it still okay if Tiffany comes over to play?" Gracie asked.

"Of course. Why don't you give her a call and let her know we're home now," John suggested as they walked into the house.

Tiffany's mother must have been eagerly awaiting Gracie's call, he thought a half hour later. She delivered her daughter to the Bennett house within fifteen minutes, promising to return for her again no later than four o'clock.

Once the girls were settled in Gracie's room, surrounded by their dolls and doll paraphernalia, John retired to his study, hoping to get caught up on some paperwork. Instead, his attention quickly drifted, his thoughts focusing on various events of the past three weeks.

Since telling Leah about the night Caro died, he'd felt as if an enormous weight had been lifted from his shoulders. No longer mired in guilt, no longer filled with self-reproach, anger, bitterness and pain, he'd been able to see, at last, the promise of a future centered on peace and happiness, centered, more specifically, on Leah.

And since making love to her that first exhilarating time, John had assumed she knew how much he loved her. He had tried to tell her, twice, and each time she had cut in to say she understood. After that, he had taken for granted that his behavior toward her in the days, now weeks, that followed had only served to reinforce her awareness of his feelings for her and just how much she meant to him.

He had been deeply grateful for her help in explaining to Gracie why he'd finally put away Caro's belongings, and he'd made sure that she'd known it. His daughter had accepted with surprising equanimity his promise, reinforced by Leah, that Caro could never be replaced in their lives and would never be forgotten, but would want them all to go on happily with their own lives now.

To John's surprise, Gracie had even said how sad she'd sometimes felt to see her mother's things still so prominently displayed in his bedroom, and he had been surer than ever that he had made the right move when he'd finally packed everything away.

John had also taken every opportunity he could find to show Leah, in the privacy of her room, how he loved her. And she'd welcomed him there with open arms each time he came to her. She had also seemed as reluctant as he to part before morning, but both of them had agreed they didn't want Gracie to see him coming out of Leah's room sleepy-eyed and sexually sated. Though John had a solution to that particular problem in mind, one he had been intending to propose to Leah for several days now.

But there had been something in her manner toward him, something he couldn't quite put his finger on. While she laughed and smiled easily, and teased him without remorse on a regular basis, and while she welcomed his lovemaking with undisguised eagerness, mating with him joyfully, he still sensed a certain reserve about her.

He often caught her with a pensive look on her lovely face, and yet she seemed determined to avoid anything even remotely resembling a serious discussion with him.

She seemed happy to be with him and Gracie, but occasionally, as she had with today's visit to Dr. Berry, she purposefully made a point of distancing herself, and he had no idea why.

Lately John had begun to wonder if he'd assumed too much where Leah was concerned. For three weeks now he thought she knew how much he loved her. For three weeks now he had thought she knew that he wanted her to be a permanent part of his life. And for three weeks now he'd thought she, too, wanted to make a life together, to marry him and be a real mother to Gracie and have more children with him and live happily ever after.

Now, sitting alone in his study with Gracie and Tiffany's voices echoing down the hallway, he realized that he had never actually said any of those things to Leah in so many words. Not because he hadn't wanted to, but because she hadn't given him the chance.

He was going to make a chance, though, John decided as he pushed away from his desk, strode out of his study and headed restlessly down the stairs. As soon as Leah returned home from her outing, he was going to get her alone and finally say to her all the things he should have said to her already.

He didn't want there to be any distance or any doubts between them anymore. And he could think of only one way to guarantee that—by being totally and completely honest with her about the hopes and dreams he had for them as husband and wife.

In the kitchen John poured a tall, frosty glass of iced tea for himself, then wandered over to the table and sat in one of the chairs. When he'd first come in with Gracie he'd noticed the pile of mail Leah had left there, but he hadn't bothered to look through it, sidetracked as he'd been by Tiffany's prompt arrival. Now he pulled the assorted magazines and envelopes, along with several postcards from Cameron and Georgette, toward him.

He read the postcards first, enjoying Georgette's descriptions of the sights she and Leah's father had seen in London, then Paris and now, apparently, Rome. Then he glanced at the magazines, all scientific journals, and set them aside. Finally he sorted through the various envelopes, mostly bills and bank or investment statements. One envelope, a thick one addressed to Leah and already slit open, caught his attention and held it as he eyed the return address with a frown.

What had Kyle O'Connor, Headmaster of Abbotsford Academy for Boys in Chicago, Illinois, sent to Ms. Leah Hayes?

Something she had taken the time to open and at least glance at before she left for her visit with Sarah in Hamilton, John thought, weighing the heavy vellum envelope in his hand as he also weighed the temptation to see for himself what it contained.

He had no right whatsoever to look at Leah's personal correspondence or invade her privacy by snooping into what was clearly her business, and her business alone. But what if Kyle O'Connor happened to be the reason for Leah's reserve toward him?

Surely it would help his cause to know what, if anything, he might be up against where O'Connor was concerned. Leah had insisted the man was just a friend, but for years she had considered *him* just a friend, too.

For several seconds longer John held the envelope, tapping it against the kitchen table as he debated with himself what to do. Finally, taking a deep breath, he withdrew the sheaf of papers the envelope contained and unfolded them. His heart thudding in his chest, his face rightfully burning with shame, he read first the short handwritten note:

Leah, I hope the enclosed will convince you once and for all of my sincerity. I want you back in my life again permanently. Please come home to Chicago and to me without any further delay. Yours always, Kyle

Suddenly feeling sick to his stomach, John next scanned the legal document O'Connor had enclosed, a petition for divorce filed by him a week ago in Chicago.

So that had been why Leah had been disappointed with O'Connor. He had been married, but sniffing after her, and when she'd broken off whatever kind of relationship they'd had, he'd decided to file for divorce as a means of winning back her affection.

Had that been what Leah wanted of O'Connor? Had she been hoping all these weeks that the man would eventually choose to end his marriage so they could be together? But then, how could she have been so intimate with *him?*

Leah had never been the promiscuous type, and John didn't think she was now. But there had been a certain holding back about her, a very definite reserve. Had it been because she didn't really love him? Was she having sex with him only because she wanted to help him heal and thought that was the best way to do it?

But they hadn't just been having sex. To John's way of thinking, they had been making love.

"Daddy, can we have some cookies and lemonade, please?" Gracie asked, bouncing gaily into the kitchen with Tiffany skipping along right behind her.

Aware that he had forgotten all about his daughter and

her friend, John hastily stuffed Kyle O'Connor's letter and petition for divorce back into the envelope and hid it under the other mail before Gracie could notice it and ask what it was.

"Sure thing, sweetie," he replied, pushing away from the table and walking over to the refrigerator. "Cookies and lemonade for two lovely young ladies coming right up."

Giggling, Gracie and Tiffany each scooted onto a chair while John welcomed the diversion of preparing an afternoon snack for them.

Anything to give him an opportunity to gather himself emotionally, he thought. More than ever, he now knew how important it was that he speak frankly with Leah about his feelings for her. He had taken too much for granted for too long where she was concerned. Now he was afraid he might have lost the battle for her heart without ever knowing a competitor had been waiting in the wings.

Well, he knew the truth about Kyle O'Connor now, and he also knew what the man wanted. But he had Leah here with him and he wasn't about to let her go back to Chicago without first telling her, once and for all, how very much he loved her and needed her in his life.

Chapter Sixteen

Leah drove slowly back to Missoula from Hamilton, her thoughts straying from the time she'd spent visiting with Sarah at the delightful little flower shop she ran single-handedly to the letter from Kyle she'd received that morning.

She hadn't expected anything at all from him, much less a copy of the petition for divorce he'd apparently filed only a week ago. She'd been surprised to see it, not so much because he'd decided to initiate divorce proceedings on his own, after all, but because he'd thought, after what he'd put her through already, that it would make a difference to her.

Obviously she hadn't voiced her feelings about resuming their relationship strongly enough to make an impact on him the one time they'd spoken since her arrival in Missoula. And she certainly wasn't going to take the time or make the effort to do so now. Her silence on the subject should speak volumes. But if he attempted to pursue the matter further with her, she wouldn't hesitate to tell him she was well and truly done with him.

Leah had known even before John had made love to her that her feelings for Kyle weren't strong enough or trusting enough to sustain a marriage. And she doubted Kyle was interested in only having her for a friend. Her biggest hope now, where he was concerned, was that she wouldn't run into him when she returned to Chicago at the end of the summer. She hated scenes of any kind, even minor ones, and preferred to avoid them at all cost.

In fact, she had done just that today by planning her visit with Sarah in Hamilton to coincide with Gracie's appointment. Leah had preferred to make a sixty-mile drive rather than witness John's reunion with the determined Dr. Dana Berry. She hadn't wanted to have to sit in the corner again and watch the doctor flirt with him as she'd done previously. Nor had she wanted to see how John responded to her obviously inviting behavior.

Even more than that, though, Leah had told herself, she'd wanted to give John the opportunity to be with another woman, one he certainly found attractive, so he could be the target of a flirtation and could respond in kind. He had dealt with the guilt, the anger and the pain of Caro's death at long last. He was finally ready now to start to develop a serious personal relationship with a woman who could not only hold her own with him, but also be comfortable coming into his life after Caro.

Dana Berry would never feel as if she was living in Caro Bennett's shadow. More than likely, the thought wouldn't even cross her intelligent and inventive mind. And if it did, she would dismiss it as a load of nonsense not worth the time it took to consider.

Just as you should, because you are intelligent and

inventive, too, and you already know that John cares for you....

Leah's hands tightened on the steering wheel as the thought zipped through her mind and settled there for further contemplation. She had to wonder what was wrong with her, intentionally sending John off to be tempted by another woman into the kind of permanent relationship that happened to be exactly what *she* wanted to have with him. But in her case there was and always would be the problem of Caro's shadow lurking in the background of her mind, as she knew it would be in John's mind.

The three of them would be tied together forever in a triangle of sorts based on the history they would always share. And at the apex of their shared history was John's love for Caro, intense and overwhelming from the moment they'd been introduced.

Leah hadn't been able to compete with that love eight years ago. And despite all the wondrous moments she had spent in John's arms over the past three weeks, she knew better than to believe she could now. Therein lay the path to false ideas.

Leah dreaded the day she would have to return to Chicago. Her heart ached unbearably at just the thought of it. But she knew the pain she would suffer when John once again wanted to revert to being just friends would be even worse. She didn't want to have to stand by a second time, smiling sweetly and agreeably when another woman, a woman like Dana Berry, caught and held his interest.

Not that she thought John was a shallow man or easily led. But whatever love he felt for her wasn't nearly as all-encompassing as the love he'd once felt for Caro.

Leah pulled into the driveway at John's house at last,

glad to be there in spite of the direction her thoughts
had taken along the way. She was glad, too, to see his
Jeep in its parking place. Whatever had happened during
Gracie's appointment with Dr. Berry, he was home now.

As she got out of her car, Leah saw Tiffany's mother
drive up to the curb. Apparently John had hosted a play
date for the little girls, she thought, smiling slightly.

He and his daughter would be just fine after she went
back to Chicago. Any doubts he'd had about his pater-
nity seemed to have disappeared completely. And along
with those doubts, so, too, had his reserve with Gracie
evaporated. With Cameron and Georgette home from
Europe to help out occasionally, Gracie in school full-
time and John's own schedule easily adjustable, he probably wouldn't need a nanny, either.

To Leah's relief, Tiffany's mother didn't linger. She
and her daughter were on their way home within
minutes.

Walking into the kitchen with John and Gracie after
waving them off, Leah saw that John had started prep-
arations for dinner. Cobs of fresh corn and russet potatoes were already wrapped in foil and stacked on a platter ready to be put on the grill, heating up on the back
patio. A bowl of ground beef and assorted jars of spices
and seasonings sat on the counter, along with a bag of
hamburger buns.

"You've been busy," she commented, her smile widening appreciatively as John offered, and she accepted,
a glass of iced tea.

"I didn't think you would feel much like cooking after the drive back from Hamilton," he replied.

Though he smiled, too, there was a hint of something
in his eyes—uncertainty and perhaps, surprisingly, the
merest hint of anger. He hadn't seemed to mind at all

earlier that she was going to see Sarah, and she didn't think that was the reason for his wary gaze. But what could it be, then?

Almost immediately, Leah's glance fell on the stack of mail that had come before she'd left for Hamilton. She remembered the opened envelope from Kyle that she hadn't bothered to put away in her room.

Had John looked at the contents of that envelope? She didn't want to assume he'd read her mail. But if he had, what difference would it make to him if a friend of hers had filed for divorce?

Of course, there was also Kyle's note asking her to come back to Chicago and to him as soon as possible. Which might, she acknowledged, work in her favor if John had seen it as she now suspected he had.

"Did you have fun with your friend Sarah?" Gracie asked. "'Cause I had lots of fun with Tiffany."

"Yes, I had fun with Sarah—lots of fun, in fact. She owns a flower shop and she puts together the most beautiful arrangements in baskets and bowls and all kinds of vases. Maybe you can go with me the next time I visit her so you can see for yourself."

"I'd like that a lot, Aunt Leah."

"Gracie, why don't you go upstairs and tidy your room while Leah and I finish making dinner?" John suggested.

Gracie looked a little surprised as she glanced at her father. She always straightened her room after Tiffany came to play. But she answered agreeably enough.

"Okay, Daddy. Then I'll come back and set the table."

"Good girl," he replied, then said to Leah, "The coals should be hot by now. Want to put the corn and potatoes on the grill?"

"Sure thing."

Glad to have a few moments to gather herself for whatever John had in mind to say to her, Leah went out to the grill and arranged the foil packets of corn and potatoes on the grill as he'd requested. She couldn't ever remember him purposely sending his daughter out of the room, so he must want to discuss something very personal, and likely regarding Kyle.

By the time she returned to the kitchen and set the now-empty platter on the counter, John had finished forming the ground beef into patties and was washing his hands at the sink. Leah's first instinct was to make some excuse and scurry off to her room. But she would have to find out what John had on his mind sooner or later, and she preferred to get it over with now than dread the confrontation any longer.

"Need help with anything else?" she asked as she paused beside him at the sink.

He finished drying his hands on a fresh towel, then without speaking turned to her, put his hands on her shoulders and drew her close for a deeply sensual kiss. When he finally raised his head, she was feeling a little breathless, not to mention a little disappointed that they wouldn't be able to finish what he'd started for several hours at least.

Still holding her tenderly in his arms, John smoothed a gentle hand over her hair.

"You do know, don't you, Leah, how much I love you?" he asked, his voice very grave.

"Hey, I love you, too," she replied in a much lighter, breezier tone, refusing to read anything really serious into his statement.

"I don't think you're really hearing me, Leah. I love you—truly, deeply and completely. I know I haven't actually said it in so many words. The few times I've tried, you've cut me off, saying you understood, and I just assumed you did. But right here, right now, I *am* saying it to you, and I am also saying that I want to marry you, to make you my wife and Gracie's mother.'' He paused and leaned back, tucked a finger under her chin and tipped up her face so that she was forced to meet his questioning gaze. "Say yes, Leah. Say yes, you'll marry me.''

Stunned into momentary silence and unable to glance away, Leah saw the same sincerity in John's pale gray eyes that she had heard in his deep, velvety voice. And she was tempted, so very, very tempted, to accept his proposal.

But she couldn't discount the little nudge of doubt that warned her he wasn't really thinking straight. She had been there for him when his guilt over Caro's death had finally faded away, and he had turned to her out of a need for solace. She had been the one most available to help him get past the last of his grief and begin to heal. That didn't mean he had to tie himself to her for the rest of his life out of gratitude, though. Gratitude, in fact, was absolutely the last thing she wanted from him, now or ever.

"I can't, John. You know that," she chided softly. "I have a life of my own in Chicago. And once you've had some time on your own to think about it, you'll realize it's best I go back to that life and leave you to get on with your life here in Missoula.''

Frowning, John took a step back and let go of her.

"Are you saying you don't love me, Leah?" he asked, sounding truly puzzled. "And you don't want to marry me?''

Much as she wanted to make him believe both those

things, she couldn't come right out and deny the true depth of her feelings for him.

"I just think it would be best for both of us if I went back to Chicago as I've been planning. In fact, it would probably be a good idea if I left within the next week or so. I never meant for you to think—"

"That you cared about me and Gracie?" he cut in, his voice scaling up several notches in obvious anger. "I've seen you with her. I've seen how much she means to you. And I've seen the look on your face when I'm inside you, loving you."

He paused, shoved a hand through his hair and glared at her in a way that threatened to destroy her hard-won resolve.

"I *do* care about you and Gracie. More than you'll ever know," she protested, her own voice rising. "But I can't stay here with you, John, I just...can't."

"Is it because of Kyle O'Connor?" John demanded. "Is he the reason you're so intent on walking out on me?"

"So what if he is?" she shot back in desperation. "Does it make any difference why I want to leave? Can't you just accept the fact that I have to go back?"

"No, Aunt Leah, no!" Gracie cried, her voice high and frightened. "You can't leave me like my mommy did. You can't!"

Stricken, Leah and John both turned to see his daughter standing in the doorway, tears streaming down her face. An instant later she turned on her heel and was gone.

"Gracie, wait," Leah called, her feet like lead as she tried to follow the little girl.

"I'll talk to her," John said. "I'll try to explain—"

The unexpected crash of the front door slamming shut startled them both into motion.

"Oh, no, she's gone outside," Leah said as she ran down the hallway, John right behind her.

What had they done, she wondered as she stepped onto the front porch and scanned the sidewalk unsuccessfully for a glimpse of the frightened child. They had been so busy arguing with each other that they'd forgotten completely that Gracie was in the house with them. Nor had they bothered to take into account how their raised voices, coupled with the words they'd spoken, would affect the sensitive little girl.

She had heard John and Caro arguing, then Caro had died. And only moments ago she had heard arguing again with a similar theme. It was easy to understand why she would now fear that she'd lose her beloved aunt in the same tragic way.

"I can't believe I was so stupid," John muttered as they moved quickly across the front lawn to the sidewalk in front of the house. "I didn't even think about Gracie."

"Neither did I. But all that's really important now is finding her and making sure she knows that nothing bad is going to happen to anyone today," Leah replied.

"I'm sorry, Leah," he said, taking her hand in his. "So very, very sorry I got angry with you."

"I'm sorry, too, John. I didn't mean to get angry, either." Threading her fingers through his, she looked up and down the street. Two doors away to the left she caught a flash of pink and turned in that direction. "This way," she said. "I think Gracie has gone this way."

What seemed like a very long time later, but couldn't have been more than a few minutes, they found the little girl huddled on the front-porch steps of the Donovan house, her head down, sobbing quietly.

"Gracie, oh, Gracie, sweetie, don't cry," Leah murmured softly, not wanting to startle her into running off again.

Letting go of John's hand, she knelt down in front of the child and gently touched her bent head. Gracie looked up, her eyes red-rimmed and her face streaked with tears.

"Aunt Leah!" she cried, throwing herself into Leah's outstretched arms.

"Please don't go away. Please, please, please don't ever, ever go away like my mommy did."

"Oh, Gracie," Leah breathed, holding the child's fragile body close. "Don't worry, sweetie. I'm not going anywhere."

"You want her to stay, too, don't you, Daddy?" Gracie looked over at John, who'd hunkered down beside Leah.

"Of course, I do," he replied.

"But you were using your growly voice," she chided, brushing at the last of her tears with one hand as she continued to hold on to Leah with the other. "You were *both* using growly voices."

"Yes, we were, and we're very sorry we did," Leah assured her, then glanced at John with a wry twist of her lips. "Aren't we?"

"Yes, we are, Gracie. We're very sorry."

"Then you have to kiss and make up," his daughter commanded.

"I think we can manage that, don't you?" John asked, reaching out to touch Leah's cheek. "Friends again?"

"Friends again," she replied, welcoming the chaste kiss on the lips he gave her.

"Okay, little girl, ready to go home again?" John asked his daughter with a sheepish grin.

"Yes, Daddy."

"How about a piggyback ride?"

"Okay."

Smiling once more, Gracie climbed onto John's shoulders and held on to his head as he stood up, groaning in a way that made her giggle with undisguised glee.

Fortunately the Donovan family had either been away or unaware of the drama on their front porch, Leah thought as she walked back to the sidewalk with John and Gracie. At least they'd been spared having to offer an explanation for the little girl's upset. And fortunately Gracie seemed reassured by her avowal, as well as her father's, that Leah wasn't going anywhere.

Not just yet, she amended to herself, though she hadn't added that caveat when she'd answered the little girl. Gracie wouldn't understand her leaving anytime soon, but with some careful preparation in the days ahead, Leah hoped she could get her to accept that she had to go back to Chicago by summer's end.

Although, after her argument with John, Leah figured the sooner she left Missoula the better for all of them. Gracie was obviously getting too attached to her, and she was getting too attached to John, and he...

Leah glanced at him as he paused on the front doorstep and swung Gracie off his shoulders amidst much teasing and laughing. John *thought* he loved her, but in truth, she knew what he really felt for her had more to do with gratitude than love, and gratitude alone wasn't enough to sustain a marriage.

She had helped him through a particularly difficult time in his life, and of course he appreciated it. But love her as she knew he'd loved Caro and probably still did?

She couldn't see any way that was possible. And if she had to settle for second-best yet again, she would rather do it as far from Missoula as she possibly could. Then she would be able to pick up the pieces and get on with her life. And freed of the burden of his gratitude to her, so would John.

"Do you think the corn and potatoes have burned to a crisp?" he asked as the three of them headed down the hallway to the kitchen.

Leah glanced at the clock on the microwave and saw that less time had passed than it seemed since Gracie had first come upon them in the midst of their argument.

"They should be all right," she said. "But you should probably put the hamburger patties on the grill now, too. That way everything should be ready at about the same time."

"Good idea," John agreed, then turned to his daughter. "Want to come outside with me or stay in here with Aunt Leah?"

"Outside with you, Daddy, so I can help you cook the hamburgers."

"I'll set the table and make a fresh pitcher of lemonade while you're out there," Leah said, hesitantly joining John at the counter as he collected the platter of hamburger patties.

Quietly, for her ears only, he spoke again.

"I *am* sorry I raised my voice to you, Leah. It really was uncalled for, whether or not Gracie was here."

"I'm sorry, too. I said some things…" She let her words trail away, knowing she would be better off letting him think she'd meant every word she'd said.

"We both did, but we can talk more later, okay?" he asked. "Because we really do need to talk some more before you make any definite decisions about the future.''

''Yes, we'll talk later,'' she agreed, letting it go at that.

There was no need to tell him right that minute that she had already made up her mind about what she planned to do. More than likely, knowing what John seemed to think he wanted that would only cause more acrimony between them. And for Gracie's sake, Leah wanted to keep the mood light and cheerful for the remainder of the evening.

They would have time enough to hash out the details of how best to arrange for her departure after the little girl was tucked in bed, fast asleep for the night. John might give her a little trouble initially, but as long as she was firm about her intentions—intentions that could include hints, however false, about her relationship with Kyle O'Connor—then she knew he would eventually give in to her wishes. He wouldn't insist on marrying her if she could convince him that her heart belonged to someone else.

Only she would know that her wishes were alleged wishes rather than real ones. But she had already given up on her real wishes ever coming true eight long years ago. It couldn't be any harder to do again now, she told herself. Because now she was older and wiser.

Chapter Seventeen

As he went through all the proper motions of grilling the burgers, eating dinner with Leah and Gracie, cleaning up the kitchen afterward, even watching a movie with the two of them that he'd rented earlier in the day, John schooled himself to be not only patient, but cheerful. He didn't want to upset Leah or Gracie any more than he already had that afternoon. And he didn't want to cause himself any more upset, either.

Leah had agreed that they needed to talk later, and once Gracie was asleep, he knew that they would. In the meantime the calmer he could force himself to be, the better for all concerned. Jumping to conclusions of any kind regarding Leah's feelings would be a big mistake, one he had already quite possibly made. He wouldn't know for sure until they were finally alone together and he could get some answers to his questions.

As he sat on the sofa in the den with Gracie cuddled

between him and Leah, watching the often humorous, sometimes poignant, story of a pioneer family unfold on the television screen, John tried to tamp down his dread of that moment. But it threatened to swell into unmanageable proportions inside him as time passed.

He had to find out how Leah really felt about him and about Kyle O'Connor. But there was a part of him that wanted to go back to the ignorant bliss he'd been enjoying since the first night he'd made love to her.

John didn't want to hear Leah say to him that she was in love with O'Connor. He didn't want to know that only the man's marriage had stood in the way of their being together, and now that he was free, or going to be free very soon, she wanted to return to Chicago and to him. And he didn't want to have to face the reality that he himself had merely been filling a gap in her life the past few weeks, and now that Kyle O'Connor wanted her back, she didn't need him anymore.

But that was exactly what he *had* to hear from Leah in order to let her go without further argument. No dissembling of any kind on her part was acceptable. She was going to have to look him in the eye and tell him she loved someone else more than she loved him.

Maybe he was an egotistical fool, overdosing on more wishful thinking than should be allowed by law. But he didn't believe it was true. And he wouldn't believe it was true until she gave him absolutely, positively no other choice in the matter.

Leah hadn't told him she was in love with Kyle O'Connor when they had first begun to argue. She had, in fact, challenged his question with one of her own. He had asked her if O'Connor was the reason she was so intent on walking out on him, and she had said, "So what if he is?'' She would have to say much more than that to finally convince him.

He had lost Leah once before because he hadn't valued her in the way he should have. But he had learned a lot in the past eight years. He valued her now, and if she didn't realize it yet, he meant to make sure she did before the night was over. And if she still wanted to return to Chicago and Kyle O'Connor, then he would have to let her go—graciously.

''That was a really good movie, Daddy,'' Gracie said, yawning hugely as the credits began to roll across the television screen.

''I enjoyed it, too,'' Leah agreed, stretching her arms over her head with seeming nonchalance, then leaning casually back against the sofa cushions again.

Glancing at her, John wondered if she had been any better able than he to pay attention to the movie. The wariness in her eyes as she met his gaze signaled that she, too, had other things on her mind.

''Sounds like you're ready for bed, young lady,'' he said to his daughter. ''Give Aunt Leah a good-night kiss so I can take you upstairs and get you tucked in.''

''Good night, Aunt Leah.'' Gracie turned to her aunt and welcomed Leah's hug and kiss. ''See you in the morning.''

''See you in the morning, too, sweetie. Sleep tight...''

''You, too, and don't let the bedbugs bite,'' the little girl replied with a giggle, completing what had become part of their nightly ritual.

John stood and swung his daughter up into his arms.

''Piggyback ride?'' he asked.

''I'm too sleepy, Daddy,'' Gracie admitted, snuggling against his chest, blinking her eyes in an effort to stay awake until he could carry her up to her room. "I'm even too sleepy for a story tonight."

"No problem," he assured her. "We can read two stories tomorrow night, okay?"

"Okay, Daddy."

After the upset she'd had earlier in the day, John understood his daughter's weariness. But she seemed to have been reassured now that he and Leah had resolved their problems and there was no longer any reason for growly voices to be raised in their house. He hoped she wouldn't have any nightmares, but all he could really do now, after the fact, was tell her again how much they both loved her as he tucked her into bed.

"I'll be back down in a few minutes," he said to Leah, making sure she knew he still expected them to have their talk.

"I'll wait for you in the kitchen," she replied with a determined tip of her chin.

They wouldn't have their discussion in her bedroom or even in the den where they could sit comfortably, or uncomfortably, close enough to touch, she indicated. In the kitchen she could easily arrange to have the table between them. And, John thought, smiling to himself as he carried Gracie up to her room, if Leah needed to put a table between them, then he must mean a hell of a lot more to her than she'd wanted him to know that afternoon.

Now if only he could get her to admit why she was so determined to go back to Chicago despite her obvious feelings for him, he would surely have won more than half the battle of keeping her here with him.

After making sure Gracie made at least a cursory job of washing her face and brushing her teeth before she put on her pajamas, John got her into bed and pulled the blankets up to her shoulders, tucking her in tight, just as she liked. He also made sure her windows were open just a bit before he came back and sat on the edge of her mattress.

"I really love Aunt Leah, Daddy," she murmured sleepily, looking up at him with drooping eyes. "Do you?"

"Yes, Gracie," he admitted, unable to be anything but honest with his daughter, especially after the scare he'd given her earlier. "I really do love her, too."

"I don't want her to ever go back to Chicago."

"Neither do I, sweetie. But she might have to, you know." Again he had to be honest with Gracie and to be fair to Leah, as well. "She can always come and visit us again, though. Because she will always be a part of our family and also one of our very best friends."

"Our very, *very* best friend," Gracie insisted as she finally closed her eyes. "Good night, Daddy."

"Good night, Gracie."

Bending over, he kissed her gently on her forehead, stood slowly and waited quietly beside her bed for several moments, until he was sure she'd fallen asleep. Then he retraced his steps down the stairs and back to the kitchen.

John thought about what he'd just said to his daughter, about how Leah might have to go back to Chicago and how he'd said it to be fair to her. And he realized that he owed her that much and more. It might not be what he wanted, but if it was what Leah wanted, what she needed, he would try to make it as easy for her as possible. He loved her enough to want her to find happiness, even if it wasn't going to be with him.

Leah was waiting for him in the kitchen as she'd said she would be, and she was sitting at the table just as he'd expected. She'd poured a glass of iced tea for each of them and set out a plate of chocolate-chip cookies. Had he not known differently, he would have thought they were getting ready to decide something as mundane as where to take their annual family vacation, rather than with whom they were going to spend the rest of their lives. Only the way she gripped her glass in both hands, knuckles white with tension, gave away her trepidation about what was to come.

In that instant John's heart ached for Leah more than for himself. He loved her so much—too much to cause her such torment. If she was that determined to leave him and Gracie, if she was that much in love with Kyle O'Connor, then he had to step aside and let her go.

Making it hard for her would only make it that much harder for himself, and he didn't want to be the source of any additional hurt or unhappiness for either of them.

"Is she asleep?" Leah asked, hesitantly meeting his gaze as he crossed the kitchen and sat beside her at the table.

"She was on her way to dreamland almost as soon as her head hit the pillow," he replied.

"She wasn't still upset about…about what happened between us earlier, was she?"

The pained look in Leah's eyes tore at John's heart. Reaching out, he gently touched her arm, hoping to reassure her.

"I don't think so."

He paused, trying to decide how much, if any, of what his daughter had said to him he should repeat. All of it, he thought, because it would give him the chance to say what *he* wanted to say.

"She told me she loved you and asked if I did, too," he continued, ignoring the way Leah's arm stiffened under his touch. "She also said she didn't want you to ever go back to Chicago, and I agreed that I didn't, either."

"Oh, John," she began, her voice filled with distress.

"Wait," he cautioned, giving her arm a squeeze when she would have pulled away. "Let me finish what I have to say to you."

"All right," she agreed, though her mouth tightened into a thin line and she glanced away, almost angrily, he thought.

"I told Gracie that I didn't want you to leave, either. But I also told her that you might have to," he said in the same quiet voice he'd used with his daughter. "And that didn't mean we would never see you again, because you could always come and visit us since you're a part of our family and also one of our very best friends."

Slowly Leah turned her head to look at him again, now seeming more surprised than angry. And somewhat puzzled, too, he realized.

"You told her that?"

"Yes, and I meant it." He moved his hand from her arm to gently caress her cheek. "I love you, Leah, and I want you to stay here with me and be a permanent part of my life, and Gracie's life, too. I know you came here for my daughter's sake. I know, too, that you put up with a lot of trouble from me for her sake, and that you would probably stay on here, at least until the end of the summer, for her sake. But I can't let you go on sacrificing your own wants and needs for her...for *us*.

"If you don't love me, Leah, as much as I love you, as much as I've always loved you somewhere deep in my heart—even when I was too besotted with Caro to think straight—then I think it really would be best if you left as soon as possible.

"Thanks to you, I've finally been able to deal with

Caro's death and the part I played in it. I know without a doubt that Gracie is my daughter in every way that counts. I can arrange my schedule at the university so that I can take care of her on my own now. I can even help her with her schoolwork. And I'll talk to her again about your leaving. I'll smooth the way with her as best I can so she won't be upset when you go. I'll make her understand that while you care a lot about us, you deserve to be with the man you really love so that you can be just as happy as you deserve to be.''

''Oh, John,'' Leah said again, taking his hand in hers and holding on to it tightly.

Before she lowered her gaze, John thought he saw a glimmer of tears in her eyes. But why would she be crying now? He had given her what she'd said she wanted when they'd argued earlier. She should be smiling, not swiping ineffectually at the tracks her tears were leaving on her pale cheeks.

''Hey, don't cry, Leah,'' he said. ''I want you to be happy.'' He tugged on her hand, adding in a teasing tone that belied his breaking heart, ''Come on now, smile for me....''

Still holding on to his hand, she bent her head and began, instead, to sob. Unable to understand what he had said to cause her such obvious desolation, John moved off his chair, lifted her into his arms and sat down again, cradling her in his lap. She clung to him, still weeping copiously, her tears dampening the fabric of his T-shirt.

All he could do was murmur softly, reassuring that everything would be all right. Once he found out what was wrong, he added silently to himself with a grim twist of his lips.

Not once in all the times he had been with Leah had John ever seen her quite so upset. She had always been so reserved around him whenever changes had occurred in her life. Stoic almost, he recalled, looking back. But now it seemed she couldn't hide her anguish, though why she was so overcome by misery he couldn't even begin to imagine.

Curled up on John's lap, holding on to his hand as if it was her only lifeline in the midst of a terrible storm, Leah willed herself to regain some control over her rampaging emotions. She couldn't seem to do it, though. She could only weep for reasons too confusing for her to sort out just yet.

She had cautioned herself to be not only calm, but also patient all through dinner and the movie they'd watched with Gracie afterward. She would have her chance to talk to John, she assured herself. She would be able to convince him it would be best for her to leave Missoula within a week or two, and to secure his help in explaining her decision to his daughter so as not to upset the little girl more than was absolutely necessary.

Based on what he had said to her before their growly voices had sent Gracie fleeing from the house, Leah had expected John to argue with her. She had also expected him to display some anger and even exasperation. But she had been prepared for such a response as she'd waited for him at the kitchen table, icy glass of tea gripped in her hands.

What she hadn't anticipated, nor would have in a million years, were the simple, honest words he'd spoken, and the undeniable sincerity she'd heard in his voice and seen mirrored in his steady gaze.

If you don't love me, Leah, as much as I love you, as much as I've always loved you somewhere deep in my heart—even when I was too besotted with Caro to think straight...

They had been so different—John and Caro. They had lived separate lives in many ways, and when Caro wanted a divorce, John had only stood in the way of it because of his own unhappy experience and his desire to spare his daughter from a similar situation. He hadn't hung on to his marriage to Caro as a way to hang on to Caro herself as Leah had wanted to believe, but, as he'd tried to tell her, to protect Gracie from what he saw as inevitable heartache.

And now that she finally understood all that, Leah thought as she gulped down a last sob and rubbed at her bleary eyes with her fingertips, John had come to the sad conclusion that *she* didn't love *him*. She had only herself to blame of course. Because that was what she'd wanted him to believe, what she'd led him to believe so he would let her go. What an awful mess she'd made of things by not believing in herself or in him.

"Here, use this," John said, pressing a clean, neatly folded handkerchief into her hand. "Then tell me, please, what I said to make you cry so hard."

"It wasn't what you said that made me cry," she replied, mopping the last of the tears from her eyes. She blew her nose, as well. Then, still holding on to John's hand, she drew a deep breath and risked looking at him. "It was how mistaken I've been about what I believed was true—about you and Caro and most of all myself. You tried to tell me so many things, so many times, in so many ways. But I refused to listen, *really* listen. I thought I had our relationship all figured out, and I was too afraid to let go of what I chose to believe because I didn't want to be hurt again."

"Leah, my lovely Leah, you must know I would never do anything intentionally to hurt you," he scolded her gently.

"Yes, I know," she told. "And you never have."

"That's why I said what I did about smoothing the way for you to go back to Chicago. I didn't want you to feel obliged to stay here with us when your heart was with someone else—someone who is now obviously free to be with you. And yes, I did look at the note and the petition for divorce your friend Kyle sent you, and I'm very sorry I did. I had no right to invade your privacy," he admitted. "Although it did help me get things straight in my mind."

"But my heart isn't anywhere else but here," Leah murmured, holding his gaze. "It hasn't ever really been anywhere else but here with you."

"Then why insist on going back to Chicago after I said I loved you and I wanted to marry you? Which, by the way, I still do," he added as an aside, then continued, a puzzled look in his eyes. "And why let me think that Kyle O'Connor was more important to you than me?"

"Because I loved you too much to stay here with you, believing as I have all along that all you really wanted from me, all you really needed from me, was my friendship," she admitted, lowering her gaze.

"You still thought that after the way I made love to you?" he demanded, though the slight smile curving the corners of his mouth took some of the sting from his words.

"I didn't want to, honestly, I didn't. But I was also afraid not to. I was here with you, day in and day out, a convenient companion of sorts. Someone you knew and trusted. Someone you felt comfortable turning to after you were finally able to come to terms with Caro's death. I just assumed that since we've always been just friends in the past, once you were feeling more yourself, you would want to go back to having that kind of platonic relationship with me again. I even thought that eventually you would be attracted to someone more like Caro, someone like Dana Berry.''

"Dana Berry?" John eyed her with genuine surprise, then smiled and shook his head. "I wasn't the least bit attracted to Dana Berry and I never would have been because she *is* so much like Caro. If nothing else, I've learned from my mistakes.''

"But you loved Caro," Leah insisted.

"I was infatuated with Caro when I first met her eight years ago. There's a difference between that and true love, honest love, love built on a foundation of genuine caring and companionship. I didn't know it then, though. I was young and much as I hate to admit it, easily led. But I know the difference now, Leah. Yes, I have always thought of you as a friend, my best friend, really. And I have treasured and always will treasure our friendship, not in and of itself alone, but because it was, is and always will be the foundation of my love for you, my true and honest love.''

Cupping her face in his hand, John bent his head and kissed her, at first gently, tentatively and then, when she sighed and relaxed against him, more deeply.

As she welcomed the sweep of his tongue across hers, Leah sighed again, accepting at last the veracity of the words he'd spoken and believing finally that she had never been or would ever be second-best in his life. She had always had her own special place in his heart, and she always would. Just as he'd had and would always have a similarly special place in hers.

"So, Ms. Hayes," he muttered, his voice darkly sensuous as he raised his head a fraction, breaking off their kiss. "Should I assume you weren't thinking straight when you refused my previous proposal of marriage?"

"Oh, no, I wasn't thinking straight at all. Not at all," she said.

"And can I also assume that if I now asked you to marry me, you would accept?" His eyes glittered with more than a hint of devilish amusement.

"Yes, you most certainly can."

"Then, my lovely Leah, will you please do me the honor of becoming my wife?"

"Yes, John," she replied, meeting his gaze steadily, willing him to hear in her words and see in her eyes all the love she had for him. "Yes, I will."

"I love you, Leah," he said softly.

"And I love you, John."

This time it was Leah who initiated their kiss. Threading her fingers through his shaggy hair, she pulled his head down and claimed his mouth with an eagerness that made him chuckle softly before he became passionately intense once again.

When at last they broke apart again, the devilish glimmer was back in his eyes, making her heart beat in double time.

"Come upstairs with me tonight, Leah," he said. "Come and let me make love to you in my bed where you belong."

She hesitated for only the merest instant, giving one last, fleeting thought to Caro. But then she remembered all that John had said to her that night, and she knew deep in her heart that she no longer stood in her stepsister's shadow. That, in fact, she never really had where John was concerned. She was a vibrant, loving and lovable woman in her own right, and she deserved all the

good things that would come to her in her new life
with John.

"I can't think of anything I would like to do more,"
she answered him, scooting off his lap, then tugging him
to his feet.

Together they walked through the darkened house, up
the staircase and along the hallway. They stopped only
to check on Gracie, who was sleeping soundly, before
they moved on.

Leah hadn't gone into John's bedroom at all since
she'd come to stay in his house. And even with her new
sense of certainty about her own special place in his life,
she again experienced a moment's trepidation as they
paused together on the threshold.

Seeming to perceive this, John turned to face her.
Hands on her shoulders, he bent his head and kissed her
again, but only lightly, reassuringly, on the lips. Then
he lifted her into his arms as if she weighed nothing and
carried her the rest of the way, settling her tenderly at
last in the center of the comforter that covered his bed.

"Don't ever doubt how much I love you, Leah," he
said simply. "You have always been first in my heart in
ways that no one else ever has."

"I won't, John. I won't ever doubt you again," she
promised as she opened her arms to him. "I love you
too much for that to ever happen."

That night John seemed to take special care with her,
going slowly, making sure he pleasured her in every way
possible. He removed her clothing one garment at a time,
pressing hot, wet kisses to each part of her body that he
uncovered before moving slowly on. And when she was
finally naked, he stripped off his own clothes, lay down
beside her and started all over gain, teasing her into a
sexual awareness unlike any she'd ever experienced.

Leah had never felt so loved. Nor had she ever felt
quite so wanton as she begged him, finally, for the release he had so determinedly withheld—the release that
only he could give her.

Even then, John moved into her slowly, stroking
deeply, only to withdraw almost completely and plunge
again with measured care. His hands threaded through
her hair, his gaze locked with hers, he teased her and
tormented her, paying no heed to her whimpered pleas.
Then, at last, he moved an arm under her hips, lifted her
into him and sent her soaring on a wave of pleasure so
intense she cried out once and then again as her body
convulsed, along with his.

"I'll get you back for that," Leah muttered a long
time later, her breaths no longer coming in gasping
pants, the hot flush on her sweat-dampened skin finally
beginning to cool as her heartbeat gradually slowed.

"Oh, yeah? And how do you plan to do that?" he
asked, sounding much too pleased with himself for her
liking.

"I would say it shouldn't be hard, but I can't because
it is—so to speak," she replied, grinning as she put a
hand on him most appropriately to make her point.

"Leah, sweetheart, how…arousing your wordplay
is…" he gasped, then moaned low in his throat.
"Though I'm not sure if it's actually arousing enough
to…"

"On its own, no," she agreed with a wicked laugh.
Then she slid down his body and put her mouth where
her hand had been before looking up at him again. "But
with a little help…"

"Oh, yes," he muttered, threading his fingers through

her hair again as she nibbled at him delicately. "With a little help you'll have *me* begging for mercy."

Much to Leah's delight, as well as John's, she soon did.

Chapter Eighteen

"How do you think Gracie will feel about our decision to get married?" Leah asked.

It was early the next morning, earlier than John usually climbed out of bed on a normal day. But today wasn't a normal day, at least not to his way of thinking. Today was the sum total of that old cliché—it was, for all intents and purposes, the first day of the rest of his life...with Leah. And he wanted to start it off right.

Leah had wanted to get up early and go downstairs to her room before his daughter awoke so she wouldn't know that her aunt had spent the night in her father's bedroom. He agreed that until they were married, they should maintain certain moral principles for the little girl's benefit, and that included the appearance of separate sleeping quarters.

But he didn't want the responsibility to be Leah's alone, especially this particular morning. He hadn't wanted her to have to creep away on her own. He didn't want her to feel diminished in any way ever again because of him.

So together they'd gone downstairs, making as little noise as possible as the sky began to lighten outside the windows with the coming dawn. And together they'd showered quickly in her bathroom, each making an effort not to give in to the temptation to make love again. Then they'd dressed casually in jeans and T-shirts and headed for the kitchen.

As Leah had set out eggs to scramble and bacon to fry, John had set up the coffeemaker to brew a fresh pot. Now, pouring the steaming liquid into the two mugs on the counter, he considered Leah's question for several moments.

"I can't say for sure," he admitted as he handed one of the mugs to Leah. "I think she will be pleased, though, very pleased. We both know how much she loves you and how much she wants you to stay here with us."

"But as her aunt Leah. That's how she's used to thinking of me."

"She's used to thinking of you as someone who loves her very much," John said gently as he slipped an arm around her shoulders and gave her a reassuring hug. "I don't imagine that's going to change once we're married, do you?"

"No, not at all," Leah replied with a smile. "I love Gracie and I love you, and that's never going to change."

"Not nearly as much as I love you," he said, bending his head to kiss her, his heart swelling with happiness.

How close he'd come to losing her! he thought. With his rash words and brash behavior he had almost succeeded in ending this new and wonderful relationship with his lovely Leah before it had barely begun. He had made her feel that she would only be second-best when, in fact, she'd always had her own special place in his heart. And now, at last, she knew it. Now, at last, her doubts had faded so that she could finally believe in the uniqueness of his love for her.

"Daddy, why are you kissing Aunt Leah like that?" Gracie asked in a giggly tone of voice. "Are you kissing and making up 'cause you used your growly voice again?"

Startled by his daughter's teasing interruption, John raised his head, exchanging a rueful look with Leah before he turned to face the little girl. She hovered near the kitchen table, an avidly mischievous look in her eyes and a naughty grin tugging at the corners of her mouth. She didn't seem to mind in the least that he and Leah had been kissing each other in a more than friendly manner. Actually, she seemed rather pleased at finding them together in a just-shy-of-compromising position.

"No, Gracie, I wasn't using my growly voice with Leah," he answered her. Drawing Leah with him, he crossed to where his daughter stood, then hunkered down in front of her, leaving Leah to sit in a nearby chair. "We were kissing because we realized that we love each other very much and we want to get married so we can all be a family together. What do you think about that?"

"Really, Daddy?" Gracie asked, her voice whisper-soft, her eyes widening in obvious surprise.

"Yes, really," he said, holding his breath, unable to gauge how she would respond next and hoping, for Leah's sake, that it would be in a favorable manner.

Gracie's gaze traveled from him to Leah, and she asked again, "Really, Aunt Leah?"

"Yes, Gracie," Leah replied, her voice wavering slightly.

She put her hand on his shoulder as if, he thought, to seek his reassurance that they were handling the situation in the best possible way. Reaching up, he covered her hand with his and gave it a gentle squeeze, which she gratefully returned.

"And then will you be like a mom to me?" the little girl continued, still eyeing Leah with the keenest interest.

"As much of a mom as you want me to be, Gracie."

"But can I still call you Aunt Leah? 'Cause you'll still be my aunt, too, won't you?"

"Yes, of course."

"Will I have a really pretty dress to wear?"

John frowned, not following Gracie's segue. Leah, too, seemed momentarily confused.

"A pretty dress to wear?" she repeated.

"For when you get married," Gracie explained patiently. "Tiffany's aunt got married to her uncle and Tiffany's mom bought her a really pretty dress to wear to the wedding. Can I have a really pretty dress to wear to your wedding, too, Aunt Leah?"

"Would you like that, Gracie? Would you like to wear a really pretty dress when your dad and I get married?"

"Oh, yes, I'd like that a lot."

"Then we'll find you the prettiest dress we possibly can," Leah promised.

"Then we can live happily ever after like in a storybook, can't we," Gracie pronounced in a tone that didn't allow for any argument.

"We can most certainly try," John replied, gathering

his daughter into his arms for a hug, making her giggle again.

"Will I have a baby sister then, too? Tiffany's going to have a baby sister, only it's still supposed to be a secret. But she told me because I'm her very best friend."

"Or maybe a baby brother?" John asked, sliding a glance Leah's way. "Baby brothers can be nice, too."

"Well, I guess a baby brother would be okay." Gracie gave John another hug, then looked at Leah. "Can we have breakfast now? I'm really hungry."

"Eggs and bacon coming right up," Leah assured her.

"I'll start the bacon," John offered as he stood up.

"And I'll set the table," Gracie said, then hesitated, a frown creasing her forehead. "What's the matter, Aunt Leah? Are you sad?"

"No, Gracie," Leah answered, smiling through the tears in her eyes as she put her arms around the little girl and looked up at John. "I'm happier than I ever thought I could be."

"Me, too, Aunt Leah. Me, too."

"Hey, count me in, too," John added, tears in his eyes, as well, his heart bursting with joy as he tucked an errant wisp of Leah's hair behind her ear.

"No, Daddy, we'll count you in *three*," Gracie declared, making them laugh as they exchanged one last loving look before getting on with the day.

There had been so much to do in the weeks leading up to their wedding. Standing in the back of the little chapel on the university campus with her father and Gracie, waiting for the organ music to swell slightly in anticipation of their measured walk down the narrow aisle, Leah couldn't believe how smoothly everything had gone.

John had helped enormously of course. But then, he'd been the one, along with Gracie, to insist on a more formal wedding ceremony. Leah had suggested something much simpler involving just the three of them, a couple of witnesses and a justice of the peace, but had been voted down immediately without any discussion. Now Leah was glad she'd gone along with John and Gracie's wishes. She'd always wanted her wedding day to be special, and they had guaranteed it would be.

Cameron and Georgette would have never forgiven her if they had eloped, either. They had been thrilled to hear that she and John had decided to marry. In fact, Leah distinctly remembered Georgette saying quite happily to her father, "I told you so," as she'd handed him the telephone when Leah called them to break the news.

They had managed to cut short their stay in Italy by rescheduling the last of her father's lectures for an earlier date. Georgette, bless her heart, had even organized a wedding shower for Leah from overseas. With the help of Susan, Debra and Sarah, she had managed to make it a surprise, as well.

There was to be a reception at the country club after the ceremony at the chapel, too, but that had been arranged by John. All Leah really had to deal with was making the necessary arrangements to move permanently from Chicago to Missoula.

She had gone back to Chicago on her own, though John had offered to accompany her. She had resigned her teaching position, sublet her apartment to a friend and stood by quietly as her personal belongings had been packed up for shipment to Montana. She had also met Kyle for a drink early on her last evening there to tell him personally about her engagement. To her relief, he had seemed quite happy for her and had wished her well without the slightest hesitation.

"Is it time now?" Gracie asked as the first strains of "The Wedding March" began to play on the organ.

"Yes, Gracie," Leah replied with a smile. "It's time for you to go. Walk slowly like we practiced, okay?"

"Okay, Aunt Leah." She patted her blond curls, then ran a hand over her pale pink satin dress, simply cut and similar in style to the one Leah wore. Leah's dress was a rich ivory, midcalf length, with a high waist and full sleeves that came to her elbow. "How do I look?"

"You look lovely, sweetie."

"You, too, Aunt Leah. You look beautiful."

Basket of pink and white rose petals in hand, the little girl started down the aisle, walking slowly as instructed. From her place at the head of the aisle, Leah saw John watching his daughter with an encouraging smile on his handsome face. Then the music swelled a little more. Gracie stopped near the altar and turned to face the back as everyone seated in the chapel rose.

"Time for you now, Leah," her father said, his voice filled with pride. "John's waiting…"

Indeed, he was. Leah saw him standing by Gracie, looking back at her. His smile widened, and as she took her first step into the future, he stood up just a little straighter. Ready and waiting for her and the wonderful life they had ahead of them…together.

* * * * *

Silhouette®
SPECIAL EDITION™

and

bestselling author
LAURIE PAIGE

introduce a new series about seven cousins—
bound by blood, honor and tradition—who bring
a whole new meaning to "family reunion"!

SEVEN DEVILS

This time, the Daltons are the good guys....

"Laurie Paige doesn't miss..."
—*New York Times* bestselling author
Catherine Coulter

"It is always a joy to savor the consistent
excellence of this outstanding author."
—*Romantic Times*

Available at your favorite retail outlet.

Where love comes alive™

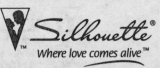

If you enjoyed what you just read,
then we've got an offer you can't resist!

Take 2 bestselling love stories FREE!
Plus get a FREE surprise gift!

Clip this page and mail it to Silhouette Reader Service™

IN U.S.A.	IN CANADA
3010 Walden Ave.	P.O. Box 609
P.O. Box 1867	Fort Erie, Ontario
Buffalo, N.Y. 14240-1867	L2A 5X3

YES! Please send me 2 free Silhouette Special Edition® novels and my free surprise gift. After receiving them, if I don't wish to receive anymore, I can return the shipping statement marked cancel. If I don't cancel, I will receive 6 brand-new novels every month, before they're available in stores! In the U.S.A., bill me at the bargain price of $3.99 plus 25¢ shipping and handling per book and applicable sales tax, if any*. In Canada, bill me at the bargain price of $4.74 plus 25¢ shipping and handling per book and applicable taxes**. That's the complete price and a savings of at least 10% off the cover prices—what a great deal! I understand that accepting the 2 free books and gift places me under no obligation ever to buy any books. I can always return a shipment and cancel at any time. Even if I never buy another book from Silhouette, the 2 free books and gift are mine to keep forever.

235 SDN DNUR
335 SDN DNUS

Name	(PLEASE PRINT)	
Address	Apt.#	
City	State/Prov.	Zip/Postal Code

* Terms and prices subject to change without notice. Sales tax applicable in N.Y.
** Canadian residents will be charged applicable provincial taxes and GST.
   All orders subject to approval. Offer limited to one per household and not valid to
   current Silhouette Special Edition® subscribers.
   ® are registered trademarks of Harlequin Books S.A., used under license.

SPED02   ©1998 Harlequin Enterprises Limited

Coming soon only from

SPECIAL EDITION™

The McClouds of MISSISSIPPI

by

GINA WILKINS

After their father's betrayal, the McCloud siblings
hid their broken hearts and drifted apart.
Would one matchmaking little girl be enough
to bridge the distance...and lead them to love?

Don't miss

The Family Plan (SE #1525)
March 2003

When Nathan McCloud adopts a four-year-old, will his sexy
law partner see he's up for more than fun and games?

Conflict of Interest (SE #1531)
April 2003

Gideon McCloud wants only peace and quiet, until
unexpected visitors tempt him with the family of his dreams.

and

Faith, Hope and Family (SE #1538)
May 2003

When Deborah McCloud returns home, will she find her
first, true love waiting with welcoming arms?

Available at your favorite retail outlet. Only from Silhouette Books!

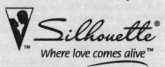

Where love comes alive™